The Big Red Bike

E.J. Tims

To Sally
Live your dreams!

Tims

Jettster Publishing

The Big Red Bike
Copyright © 2009 by E.J. Tims.

All characters are based on real life experiences of the author.

First Printing 2009
Printed in the United States of America.

Drawings by Hannah B. Mitchell
Payson, UT

Cover picture by Bella Bean Photography
www.bellabeanphotography.com
Pictured on front cover: Mason Gibb

Thanks to my editor MJ Pangman
for her hard work and support.

ISBN 0-07-212575-6
Jettster Publishing
158 East. 1170 South
Payson, Utah 84651
www.mybigredbike.com

I would like to give a very special thanks to my wife Debra and my son Jett.

Their support and help have made this all possible.

In Memory of Larry

I thank and praise God for every memory of Larry. He
was a stalwart friend that was full of fun and life. His
memory will always be a part of me and has helped to
guide my life after all these years!
A single candle can illuminate an entire room. A true
friend lights up an entire lifetime.

CONTENTS

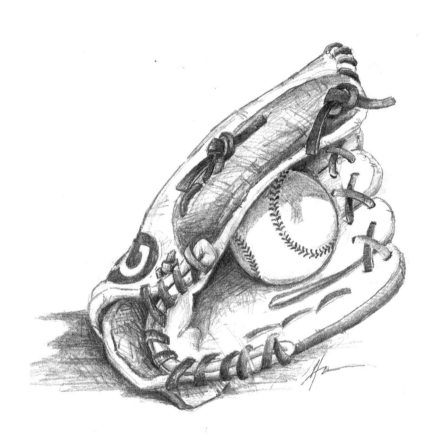

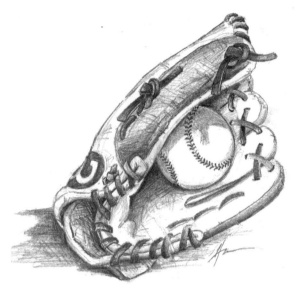

Chapter 1
School's Out

The hands on the big round clock over the classroom door moved like they were stuck in glue—the same glue that kept everyone's eyes watching with excitement. Each tick felt like it took an hour. Finally, as the last 10 seconds worked their way off the clock, we slid our feet out from under our desks and got ready to run.

The bell let out a loud ring. I could barely hear it over the screams and yells—including my own—as we bolted for the door. The sound of desks being pushed out of the way and feet scraping across the floor was deafening as a herd of bodies moved all at once toward the door. Our teacher, Miss McGonagal, scrambled behind her desk in a last ditch effort to save her life.

We worked our way down the hall and into the bright, spring sunlight. I put my hand over my eyes to cut down the glare and glanced around to find my friends. The sun was working hard to burn the last wispy clouds from around the peaks of the Rocky Mountains visible from the schoolhouse in Layton, Utah. The cool spring breeze ruffled my hair and filled my senses with the smell of freshly cut grass.

It was May 1955. I was 9 years old—a tall lanky boy with dark brown hair that went in every direction except where I wanted it to. The spring sun had already kissed my face with a few new freckles that would undoubtedly spread across my nose and cheeks as the summer progressed. I was more bone than muscle but I could hold my own when it came to sports. The summer ahead would undoubtedly provide plenty of opportunity for neighborhood baseball, basketball, and football. I wasn't the smartest kid in school and books weren't my thing but none of that mattered now—summer was here and we were free.

My friends and I stood at the top of the school steps looking down at the throngs of kids running toward buses, bikes, and the few parked cars where parents were waiting.

Our bikes were scattered in a mass of wheels and handlebars that lined the side of the school. Only a few were neatly standing with their front wheels tucked into the rails of a bike rack. Some were propped up with kick stands but most of them were lying on the ground piled on top of each other.

In spite of the mess, it was easy to find my bike. Mine was the pile of junk I called *"The Monster."* Its life had been one of hard knocks. It was a four-time hand-me-down that had been used and abused by my three older sisters. After all the paint jobs it had received it must have weighed 10 pounds more than it originally did. You could see all the colors it had been painted like a rainbow through the deep scratches on the fenders and frame—red, blue, white. My dad had

painted it green on my 5th birthday and I had used
it harder than any of my sisters. Now the green
was wearing through.

The fenders on *The Monster* had large pockets
of rust everywhere. They had been wired on with
bailing wire where the screws should have been
and they were bent and twisted so that the tires
rubbed against the frame.

The handle bars were no better. (You should
try riding a bike when the right handle bar is two
inches lower than the left one.) Most of the chrome
had peeled off and rust had set in everywhere
there was a bare spot. The grips had worn off
long ago and I had rummaged through my dad's
toolbox to find a roll of electrical tape which I had
wrapped around the ends of the handles to give
me something to hold onto.

The only thing that wasn't worn out on my bike
was the new black seat. It was bolted onto the rod
that went into the frame but the clamp that held it
was so old and worn out that it didn't stay up where
I needed it to be. My knees were practically in my
chest as I worked the pedals. The seat also spun
around because the clamp that was supposed to

hold it in position had come off years ago. My old green, hand-me-down wreck was the laughing stock of the neighborhood. Thank goodness my friends didn't make fun of me—at least not to my face.

We were all in the same grade, Larry, Lonnie, Billy, and I. We did everything together and we planned on spending as much time together during the summer as possible.

Larry was my best friend. He had that "little boy" look that all the grown-ups loved. They would ruffle his hair and comment about how cute his freckles were across his nose. (His hair was always cut short because when it was long it went everywhere—like mine.) Everyone liked Larry. He was the "nice guy." He was a little shorter than the rest of us and the slightest bit pudgy, but that never made any difference when it came to sports. Larry could outplay us all at basketball. He was quick and he made everything about basketball look easy. He had great moves and would leave us standing, wondering where he'd gone. Larry lived down the street and around the corner from me. Billy lived across the street from Larry.

Billy was a lot meaner than the rest of us—a bully. He was bigger, stockier, and a lot stronger. He was certainly the toughest of us all, and he made sure we knew it. When Billy was around we were all braver—probably because if we didn't stand our ground he would have punched us out. You never wanted to get into a fight with Billy. That would have been like riding your bike into the side of a big tree and thinking you were going to come out all right. I suppose one of the reasons he was our friend was because we didn't want him as our enemy. But sometimes it was rough. When we played football he would run over us like a lawn mower chopping up weeds. Often that was the way he treated us too. He was the lawn mower and we were the weeds.

Lonnie was the quiet one. He never said much but he was always ready to do anything that sounded like fun. Lonnie lived about a half mile away on the other end of the neighborhood.

As we stood there together watching everyone scatter, you could tell Lonnie had something on his mind. He was so soft spoken that it was hard to know whether to encourage him or to just let it go. Finally, he blurted it out.

"My dad is building us a surprise for the summer." He got this devilish smile on his face and a gleam in his eyes. His dad was always building something fun. "Told me to keep it a secret 'til it's done."

Now, Billy was the one with the devil in his eye. Looking at the two of us, he said, "We'll sneak up and see what's going on. What do you guys think?" We grinned at each other and knew we would find a time to visit Lonnie's garage and take a look.

We pushed our way through the other kids, located our bikes from the pile and, side by side, we crossed the road as we headed toward our small neighborhood. Sugar beets and corn were just starting to peak through the ground. They created a blanket of green along both sides of the road.

Just then a fighter plane from the nearby Air Force Base flew overhead. No one could hear anything but the roar of the plane for 10 or 15 seconds. That was something we had all gotten used to. It happened several times a day and it made the windows rattle all over town—especially at home. Our house was right in line with the runway so when the big C-124 cargo planes flew over, my bed would bounce all over the place.

Nearly everyone in our neighborhood worked at the Air Force Base. And if they didn't work there they either owned or worked on the nearby farms. There were lots of migrant workers too. Many of them stuck around after the harvest. There were some pretty tough Hispanic kids including a small group that was always looking for a fight. I knew that one day Billy would take them up on their challenge and I hoped that when that day came, we were all as ready as Billy seemed to be.

The whole neighborhood looked the same. Each house was the same design—compact living room, kitchen, one bathroom, two bedrooms, and a one-car garage. One house had the garage on the left side and the next house had the garage on the right. I guess they thought that would make the houses look different. But it was easy enough to tell that they had just flipped the blueprint over. The other thing they did to try and make the houses look different was to change the color of the bricks. Under the circumstances, everyone did their best to distinguish their home from the others. Flower gardens and trees were a big deal. Some families painted the trim differently or they painted their garage door a different color. But all in all, it was a pretty bland neighborhood.

We pulled into Larry's yard, dropped our bikes on the ground, and ran into his house. His mom was in the kitchen with her dark blue apron around her neck. A small yellow and chrome table occupied the middle of the kitchen. Four matching chrome chairs surrounded the table. Over the door to the living room was the clock his mom had received for her birthday. It was a black cat with the clock in its belly; the tail and the eyes moved back and forth as it ticked off the seconds. And sitting on the window sill over the sink was their big black cat, (the real thing) lying in the sun keeping an eye on the bowl of scraps Larry's mother saved by the sink.

The smell of freshly baked cookies filled the air making my mouth swim with saliva.

My eyes followed my nose toward the table. There, on a big plate, was a pile of chocolate chip cookies waiting for us.

"Hi boys. Come in and sit down." Larry's mother moved to the fridge and pulled out a brown jug full of ice-cold milk. Opening the cupboard, she found glasses for each of us as we all sat down. Larry's little brother was two minutes ahead of us. He sat there holding a big cookie in one hand and a glass of milk in the other—chocolate smeared all over his mouth.

I looked up into Larry's mom's face with a grin and said, "Thanks for the cookies; they smell *so* good."

She just smiled and ruffled her fingers through my hair. She stepped back toward the counter as we poured the milk and made pigs of ourselves. Then, after putting our glasses in the sink, we all said, "Thanks" and headed out the door.

"You boys stay close to home and stay out of trouble."

As we waved good bye, Larry grabbed his baseball glove and one for Lonnie. He lingered just long enough for his mom to reach out and pat him on the backside. "Be back for dinner son."

"Okay mom," he replied as the screen door banged shut.

We shot across the street to Billy's house. His parents both worked and the key to the house was under a pot next to the front door. Lifting the pot and grabbing the key, he opened the door and ran inside. In seconds, he was back with his baseball glove. That's all he needed. Sliding the key back under the pot, he joined us as we headed toward my house—Larry with two baseball gloves hanging from the handlebars—Billy with his glove tucked under the spring-loaded carrier above the front tire.

If we were not on our bikes headed somewhere during the summer, we were playing basketball in the school parking lot or football and baseball in my front yard. That's what we had in mind for today. My yard was the corner lot—the biggest on the street—and the perfect place for a game of baseball.

Both my parents worked at the Air Force Base, so no one was home. I had three older sisters but two of them were already married and Virginia was almost 17. She was always with her friends or working. She was never home. I was practically an only child.

We rummaged through the garbage can and found some pieces of cardboard to use for bases. The neighbors saw us and they ran across the street to join in. Jody came with his big brother—then all three of the Jones brothers—Phil, Mickey and Sammy.

Playing baseball in the front yard was always so much fun. Today was no different. We made fun of each other when we missed the ball and we pushed each other off the bases to make the play. Someone was always falling into the big bush at the edge of the yard, trying to make the "catch of the day." We were full of energy and so happy to be out of school.

All too soon the neighbors were called home for dinner. My friends and I picked up the cardboard bases and went to the maple tree at the side of my house. Shadows were beginning to creep across the lawn as the sun moved lower in the sky. This left a cool spot underneath the tree for us to talk about our plans for the night.

Now that school was out, the four of us planned on spending almost every waking hour together. We could always find something fun to do or some kind of trouble to get into. (Don't get me wrong. We were all good kids and if we did get into any trouble it was because we were together. When I say "trouble" I'm not talking about real trouble— just the kind of mischief 9-year-old boys can find in a small, farm town.) Sometimes we would sneak off on our bikes after everyone was asleep. Other times, we raided the watermelon patch in Mr. Gerber's garden. But what I really loved most was sneaking into the Davis Drive-in Theater to watch movies from the cover of the trees behind all the cars.

Lonnie sat cross-legged on the grass that had grown especially thick under the maple tree. Leaning back against the trunk of the tree, he reached down and pulled up a long grass stalk. He peeled back the course outer shaft and began to chew on the soft new growth inside. For the second time today there was a gleam in his eyes.

"I want to catch some more pigeons," he said. "You guys want to help me?"

Larry looked at me and I looked at Billy. We all shrugged our shoulders.

Larry asked, "Don't you already have about a hundred pigeons? How many pigeons do you need? And where are we going to get more anyway?"

Lonnie smiled. "My grandpa's barn. There are tons of them there at night. We just need to catch 'em, and I know how."

Billy jumped to his feet brushing the grass from his pant legs. "I'm in. When do we leave? I just need to tell my folks where we are going."

Lonnie leaned forward onto his knees and pushed himself to his feet. Smiling at us so that he showed off his chipped front tooth, he said, "Just after dark. Let's meet at my house. We can ride together. I've got flashlights and everything we need."

We exchanged our secret handshake, bumped elbows, and everyone headed home for dinner.

Chapter 2
Lonnie's Secret

I sat down with my parents for dinner. The kitchen was just big enough to hold the fridge, a stove, and a small table with four chairs. Mom served homemade bread with a bowl of ham hocks and white beans. That's what we lived on for supper at least two nights a week. My parents both worked hard but we didn't have a lot in those days.

I didn't mind the meal. I had gotten used to it. I had learned a long time ago: *You get what you get and you don't throw a fit.* That's what my father told me every time I complained—so complaining was pretty much out of the question. I had learned to accept things as they were and to be happy with them. I had also learned to enjoy a full stomach, no matter how it got that way. And besides, my mom's homemade bread was incredible. I never complained about eating that.

Mopping the last bit of my meal up with a piece of bread, I headed out the door. Mom asked me where I was going in such a hurry and I wasn't sure she heard my reply. My mouth was full and the door slammed shut behind me.

Jumping on *The Monster* I headed off to Lonnie's. My hands stuck to the tape I had wrapped around the handle bars and it made them all gooey. Every time I rode my bike these days I had a sick feeling in the pit of my stomach. Especially now that summer was here, I longed for a bike I could ride with pride.

This was the first time I had ever been on a pigeon hunt. Lonnie's dad had helped him catch lots of pigeons. Then he had traded and bought a few more from older kids around town. He had dozens. I wasn't sure why.

It was getting dark when I arrived at Lonnie's. He lived in a house like all the others—only his was made of ugly yellow brick. Seeing it made me glad my house was made with red brick—even though the houses were all the same. Lonnie was sitting on the front steps waiting for us. Larry and Billy hadn't arrived yet so I laid my bike on the lawn. The back wheel was still spinning and it rubbed against the frame making a scraping noise each time the tire hit the frame. Lonnie looked at it and shook his head.

"Don't you think that bike needs to be retired?" We both laughed, but his comment made the feeling in the pit of my stomach worse.

"You know how bad I want a new bike," I explained, "but there's no way my folks can afford it right now. Maybe someday."

I stuck out my foot and gave the bike a good kick. It slid back as the pedal dug into the grass. The back wheel stopped spinning. For a moment it was quiet. I thought about how all my friends had new or fairly new bicycles except me. I wanted a new bike in the worst way. It was all I thought of when I was alone. Then I remembered my dad's words, *You get what you get and you don't throw a fit.* A new bike was out of the question. That was all there was to it.

Lonnie broke the silence. "Where are those guys? They are never late."

Just then, Billy and Larry came walking around the side of the house pushing their bikes beside them. Billy had that mischievous look on his face. "Just checking out the garage to see what your dad's been up to," he blurted out. "You know I can't stand secrets."

Larry was smiling beside Billy. They put down their bikes and sat down on the steps with us. Billy leaned over and picked up one of the flashlights and began turning it on and off.

Lonnie, with a disappointed look on his face, turned towards them both. "Well? What did you see?"

"Everything," smirked Billy. "That is so neat! When will it be done?"

I jumped up running around the corner to look in the garage. They followed me. Sitting on the workbench was the frame and all the parts for a gas engine go-cart. The frame had been welded together and the engine (from an old lawn mower) was bolted in place. Lonnie's dad had rigged a fan belt from the engine to a pulley on the back axle. There was a small wooden seat mounted in the center of the cart. It looked like all it needed was the steering wheel and the wheels. It was awesome.

"Wow, Lonnie, this is neat," I said as I ran my fingers across the steering wheel lying on the workbench. "When will it be ready to ride?"

Lonnie groaned, "My dad can only work on it when he has time. He works two jobs right now so he can only work on it on Sundays. But when it's ready, we will have some fun on this one."

We all started to argue over who would take the first ride, and for the first time in my life, I heard Lonnie raise his voice.

"STOP IT!" He yelled as he stomped his foot. "*I* get the first ride—*and* the second *and* the third if I want. Then, if you're nice, you can all have a ride *after* that."

Billy stepped back with a look of surprise on his face and said, "Well Lonnie, you have some cahonies after all."

We all laughed and turning off the light, we closed the garage door. We could hear Lonnie's pigeons cooing in the big cage he had built for them behind the garage. That reminded us why we had come.

Chapter 3
Pigeon Hunt

Back on the front porch Lonnie filled us in on the pigeon hunt. "I think I must have only boy pigeons because they don't lay any eggs and all they do is eat and poop on the floor," complained Lonnie. "I need a few 'girl ones.' That's why we're hunting for more birds tonight. I'll show you what to do when we get there."

We picked up our bikes and pushing them out of the yard, we headed up the small hill toward

Lonnie's grandpa's farm. Everyone was soon way ahead of me because there were a few missing sprockets on the crank of my bike. If I pushed down too hard on the pedals the chain would come off. I wasn't about to have that happen tonight. For one thing, it really hurt when the bike stopped that fast. I either went flying over the top of the handlebars or I was slammed down onto the bar of the frame—neither was something I wanted to experience tonight.

Moonlight filled the night sky. Deep shadows cast by huge trees along the country road left me with that feeling that something or someone was watching. A barn owl hooted and a sudden breeze ruffled the leaves in the trees. The sound of my back wheel rubbing against the frame was comforting—in an odd sort of way—as I rode down the dusty country road alone. I was relieved when I could see my friends finally slowing down way ahead of me.

As I caught up, I could see the outline of the big white barn. We crossed over a wooden bridge and sped into the yard in front of the barn. We stopped in front of the big sliding doors and leaned our bikes against the barn wall.

"Shh!" silenced Lonnie. "We need to be quiet from now on. If we make too much noise we'll spook the birds." Lonnie untied a gunny sack from his handlebars. Inside were the flashlights.

What I didn't know and what I was about to find out was that it took lots of nerve to catch pigeons at night in a big barn. The pigeons were roosting high in the rafters. You had to climb up and crawl across the beams in the rafters to where the birds were. Then you had to shine a light in their eyes and grab them at the same time and put them in a gunny sack. And another thing... at this time of the year the barn was mostly empty because the first hay cutting was still in the field. It was a long way down to a hard dusty floor.

"Be quiet. Don't spook the birds," Lonnie scolded again.

We walked to the far end of the barn. He opened a small door leading into the milking stalls and we went down a walkway bumping into each other in the total darkness. My eyes started to adjust but it was still so dark that I could barely see my own hand in front of my face. I could hear something rattling next to me and then I realized it was Billy's teeth. I squeaked a little laugh and Billy grabbed my arm so hard that it hurt. That was enough to let me know I'd better keep my mouth shut.

The old barn floor groaned under our weight as we made our way across it. Each step disturbed aging cow manure that rose in puffs of dust around us and intensified the smell of the old barn. Holding his hand over the end of the flashlight, Lonnie turned it on and whispered for us to follow him. Against the wall in the corner was a ladder nailed to the side of the barn. It was so old that the steps had deep grooves in them. My eyes followed it up until it disappeared into the darkness.

Lonnie opened the gunny sack and pulled out the other flashlight. He turned to me and whispered through his teeth, "Take this light and we'll go up the ladder. You go first." He pushed me toward the ladder. The first step creaked as my shaking foot settled on the step. I was several rungs up before I realized I had been set up by my friends, but it was too late.

My heart was already beating out of my chest. With the flashlight tucked inside my pocket, I put one hand in front of the other. Moving slowly, I disturbed thick wads of dust on each step of the ladder as I ascended. At one point, I stopped and looked down. I couldn't see a thing below me ...but then I couldn't see anything above me either. A sudden feeling of panic filled every ounce of me as I realized what I was doing. I started to shake all over but there was no way to turn back. Lonnie was right behind me.

"What am I doing this for?" I whispered back down the ladder at Lonnie. "I don't even like these stinky birds anyway." Lonnie just pushed on my leg to keep me going.

I had been climbing forever when I hit my head on a large wooden beam that was more than a foot across. It almost knocked me off the ladder. I held on tight while the stars cleared from around my head. With a throbbing head and a dizzy feeling I reached out to feel where I was. Just then, Lonnie placed his hand over the end of the flashlight and turned it on for a few seconds—just long enough for me to see where I needed to go. Pulling myself onto a large wooden beam, I wrapped both legs around it and then locked on with both arms.

I wanted to just sit there and let my head quit hurting—and see if my heart would stop beating so rapidly but Lonnie kept pushing me forward along the beam. I tried to kick him each time he urged me forward but he kept prodding me along. Little by little we inched our way toward the center of the barn.

Once there, I could hear pigeons rustling ahead of us and making light cooing noises. Lonnie said they wouldn't fly if we didn't scare them too much because they couldn't see at night. He turned on his flashlight and directed it along the beam. The amount of dust we had kicked up was enormous and it was visible in the beam of light. I also saw pieces of straw fall into the darkness below us. For the first time I got a good look at where I was. Fear took hold of me even more. I put my arms around the beam and dug my fingernails in. I tucked my face so close to the beam that the smell of old wood and dust made me choke. All I could see below me was darkness.

Lonnie directed the light towards the floor where Billy and Larry were looking up at us.

From this far up they looked like three-year-old kids. We were at least 40 feet from the floor—at night—in the dark. *"This is really crazy,"* I thought to myself. But even that far away I could see "brave" Billy's teeth grinning in the dark. A few minutes earlier those same teeth had been rattling. Now they gleamed up at me and I could hear Billy chuckle as he watched me hug that big piece of old wood. What he couldn't see were the chunks of wood that had been pressed underneath my fingernails as I held on for dear life!

Lonnie poked me again, whispering, "Look." He moved the light slowly along the beam and we could see several sets of tiny eyes in the rafters. "There they are," he whispered. Obviously, I was not getting down until we had caught some of those stupid birds.

"Get going," Lonnie prodded, "and let's get what we came for."

I took a long deep breath and pulled myself along the beam in the direction of the eyes I had seen. When I thought I was getting close, I stopped. Lonnie turned the light on and I knew what I had to do. I grabbed a pigeon with one hand while holding onto the beam with the other. Then I reached around and located the sack hanging on my belt. After several tries, I found the opening and dropped the pigeon in. I had really caught one! Unfortunately, *one* was not enough for Lonnie. We moved toward the next pigeon about 10 feet further along the beam. Eventually, we ran out of birds and beam. I couldn't have been more relieved.

I had no idea that getting back down would be harder than getting up, but it was. Trying to go backwards along that beam was one of the hardest things I have ever done—even to this day. My hands were shaking, my heart was pounding, I had a headache, and dirty sweat was literally rolling off my whole body. My shirt was soaked by the time I reached the ladder and started to go down.

The best part now, was that I could use the flashlight to see where I was going. I reached in my pocket, pulled it out and turned it on. I looked up at the beam where I had been and I started to sweat all over again. Then I looked down to see my so-called friends laughing at me. Larry was chuckling but Billy had lost it. He was bent over, laughing his guts out.

I was still far from being on solid ground and it seemed like it took forever for me to get down the ladder. As I worked my way down, I had plenty of time to come to the realization that it was *me* who was the fool. *Never again*, I repeated to myself over and over.

Finally at the bottom, I sat down on the floor and tried to breathe normally. It all caught up with me and I was suddenly sick. I had to put my head between my knees to keep from losing my dinner. When I was finally all right, I untied the sack hanging from my belt. There were actually five pigeons flapping around inside! I couldn't believe what I had done ...and I had a few words for Billy.

"You are so mean, Billy," I spat out. "I'd like to see you climb up there and even get one pigeon. You'd never make it."

He kicked some straw towards me with his foot and just shook his head. "Let's get out of here. I've had my laugh for the day. No, I believe I've had my laugh for the week—maybe even for the month."

I don't know why I didn't tell everyone right then and there that Billy was so scared his teeth were rattling—before there was anything to be scared about! But something told me I was better off keeping my mouth shut, so I did.

Outside, the moon was already moving behind the line of trees to the West. We grabbed our bikes and started down the hill. The cool breeze dried my shirt and hair quickly. By the time I got home I was kicking myself—both for being such a fool and for being so afraid. Nevertheless, my last words to myself as I dropped off to sleep were, *Never again!*

I fell asleep quickly and had a dream. I had dreamed the same dream many times:

I was effortlessly riding a brand new bike—literally floating across town as I visited my friends one by one. Each time I arrived at a friend's house he gazed at my bike with amazement and envy. Each friend begged me for a ride.

Chapter 4
Hunt & Run Fun Day!

With my first (and last) pigeon hunt behind me, I "officially" started my summer vacation the next morning. A group of fighter planes took off early from the Air Force Base and literally shook me out of bed. From my bedroom window I could see the light summer breeze blowing the leaves on the big maple tree outside. The sunlight glanced off the moist leaves and sent little flashes of light through the window making tiny rainbows dance on the wall. The birds were already busy snatching butterflies and I decided it was time I was up too. I rolled out of bed, slipped my dusty coveralls on and headed down the hall to the kitchen. My mom was already shaping dough into large loaves of sweet-smelling bread. On the table were two freshly baked rolls, still hot and smothered with homemade strawberry jam. Mom smiled at me as I put one whole roll in my mouth and grabbed the other.

Saturday was chore day—the day I had to cut the lawn, weed the garden, and take care of other items on a list that had my name on it. The list was posted on the front of the fridge every Saturday morning. My mom saw me glance in that direction.

"It will be up there on Monday," she smiled at me. "Just enjoy the day. Stay out of trouble and be home for lunch."

I thanked her and bolted out the door. I found my bike where I had left it the night before leaning against the garage. Besides being chore day, Saturday was also what my friends and I called our "hunt and run fun day." It was the way we had discovered for getting our fill of sweets. With mom and dad both so financially bound, there was no room for an allowance for me. If I wanted anything extra, I had to figure out a way to get it myself. That's what "hunt and run fun day" was all about.

I pulled out of the yard and as I rounded the corner, the seat on my bike swiveled in the opposite direction. I should have been prepared for it because it happened all the time, but today in my hurry, I lost my balance. I over corrected, twisting the handlebars too far in the opposite direction and down I went. One of the kids across the street saw me fall and laughed. I should have been used to that too. Kids were always laughing at me and my old bike.

Dusting myself off, I rode to pick up Larry, Billy, and Lonnie. Then sitting on an old bench under a tree by a vacant house we reviewed our assigned routes—not that we needed to. We had been doing this every Saturday, spring through fall, since we could ride our bikes to town. I took the first two streets in the neighborhood; Billy took the next two streets; Lonnie always got farmers row; (he had relatives that owned some of the farms); and Larry took the last two streets. That was pretty much our little neighborhood.

We were looking for loot and our treasure was empty soda pop bottles. The big quart bottles were worth 5 cents each and the little ones were worth 3 cents. We spread out and went to work. Garbage day was Monday so we could sort through nearly a week's trash if we wanted to. Thankfully, most people left their bottles out for us. Mrs. Wilson always set her bottles on the back porch. She was my first grade teacher. Whenever I saw her in the yard she would stop me and chat about reading books. I always figured it was worth the time because she usually left me five or six bottles.

By 10:00 a.m. we had finished our assigned routes and we were sitting in my front yard to count up our bounty. With paper and pencil we added up our total. We played "thumb wars" or "rock, paper, scissors" to see who would get the odd penny or two that we couldn't divide equally between us. Then, we were off to Dansie's—the small grocery store in town.

Years earlier there had been an old train that ran from Salt Lake City to Ogden. When it quit running, they took the rails out and left the Bangerter trail. It was a great way for us kids to travel without going on any main roads. The only problem for me was that it was covered with rocks. The tires on my old bike were so bald they were shiny. I was always afraid that if I hit anything sharp my tire would blow out. So once again, my bike slowed me down and my friends had to wait for me when they reached the turnoff onto Main Street in Layton.

Our first stop was Jerry's house. Jerry owned a beautiful black stallion and Lonnie always brought sugar cubes to give him.

"Why do we always have to stop here every time we come this way?" Billy grumbled.

Lonnie didn't pay any attention to Billy. As soon as the big black stallion saw us he trotted toward the fence. He knew Lonnie had a treat for him and he nuzzled Lonnie's hand as he took the sugar. Lonnie reached through the fence rubbing his head and ears. Then dusting off his hands, he got on his bike and we all headed down the road—being careful not to jostle the bottles too much. We had wrapped the bottles in newspaper but we still had to be careful not to break or chip them as we rode.

The thing I enjoyed most about this ride was the chance to pass the new Schwinn Bicycle shop. I slowed way down so I could look at the new bikes lined up inside. The owner, Mr. Paterson, went to our church so when he saw me he always waved. Today as I approached the bike shop I wished, like I had never wished before, that *The Monster* would turn into a new bike like the ones I could see through the window. I glanced back over my shoulder and made a promise to myself as I passed. *Somehow; some way, I will have a new bike.*

Dansie's Market was just down the road. To us kids it had everything—sporting goods, meat and groceries, guns and knives, a bakery, and best of all—candy. Mr. Dansie was cleaning up the produce when we arrived. He smiled as we marched through the front door with our arms full of pop bottles.

The old country store was filled with smells. (Just thinking about them brings back memories.) Mrs. Dansie was baking upstairs. The smell of cinnamon rolls filled the store. She was known throughout the whole county for her sticky buns.

On top of the counter under a glass cover were samples of her famous finger-licking baked goods.

Mr. Dansie lifted the cover and offered us a sample. "Have a taste, boys. It's been a long bike ride for you this morning." He continued. "I was wondering if I would see you boys today—being that school is out and I have all those new candy bars that just came in here yesterday!"

"Yes sir, Mr. Dansie," we all said together.

"We were wondering if you were bringing in any of the new ones for us?" Larry asked. He looked down the aisle to the candy shelves. There were three new candy bars we had never seen before.

Mr. Dansie pulled out a grocery cart and helped us gently put the bottles in it. We went back outside to get the rest. He then carefully inspected each bottle for cracks and chips around the top before placing it in another basket behind him. Four pairs of hungry eyes watched as each bottle made its way into the "keeper" basket. It never failed that one or two bottles would be damaged from the ride to the store. We all felt the loss when he shook his head and put a bottle aside.

When the total was reached, Mr. Dansie asked, "Divide it the same way boys?"

"Yes," we all answered in unison as our heads bobbed up and down.

Money in hand, our *hunt and run fun day* was about to pay off. Whoever had won the odd penny always teased the other three as we made our way along the 10-foot candy counter. My eyes were on the lookout for new items but I had some old favorites too. I loved the lemon drops, the Big Daddys, the pop rings, and the penny candy. You could get four candies for a penny. (Back then, almost everything at the candy counter was just a penny, except the big candy bars. Nothing was over 5 cents.)

When we had picked out our share of sweets, Mr. Dansie bagged the candy in little paper bags with the store name on them. Jubilantly, we went out the swinging front doors into the sun. Next to the store was a small tree with a patch of grass underneath—just big enough for the four of us to sit in the shade and eat the fruits of our labors.

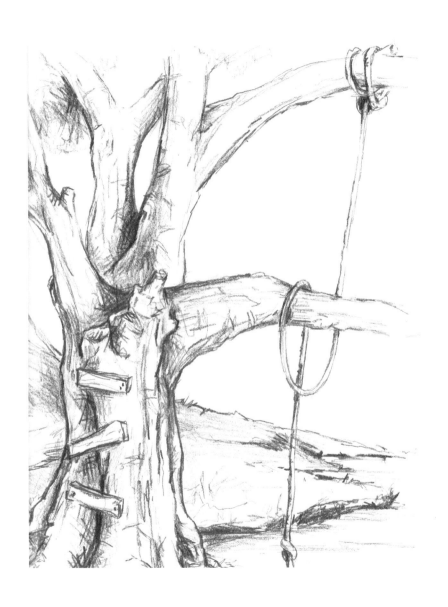

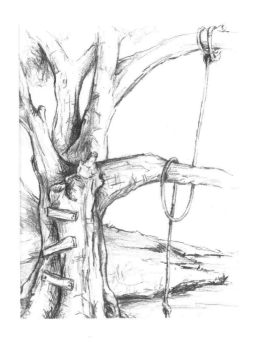

Chapter 5
The Swimming Hole

Larry pulled a piece of red licorice from his bag. Billy licked chocolate from his fingers. I had a lemon drop in my mouth but I was far away dreaming about a new bike. We hadn't been in the shade too long before Larry decided he had had enough. He wiped the sticky licorice from his fingers and declared, "I think it's time we took a good swim."

I jumped up and without a word I rolled up my bag of candy and put it in the basket on the front of my bike. I reached over as Larry mounted his bike and gave it a tap with my foot. "Great idea," I said. He caught himself just in time to keep from falling over.

We left Dansie's Market and headed down Main Street toward the old Bangerter trail. I slowed down in front of the bicycle shop and came to a complete stop. My friends were used to me lagging behind so I took my time and gazed in through the front window to see the row of new bikes.

I could see a man with his daughter inside. Her long pig tails flopped back and forth as she went from bike to bike considering every option. She climbed on a red bike—then a yellow one. I noticed the big smile on Mr. Paterson's face as she nodded her head in a *yes*.

That should be me getting a new bike, I said to myself. I was the one who really needed one. But as quickly as I heard the words in my head, I realized how happy the little girl was. I knew how she must feel to be getting a new bike and I decided to let go of my own gloom and be happy for her.

I hurried to catch up with my friends. They had stopped at Jerry's. Lonnie had just finished giving the big black stallion another piece of sugar when I pulled up.

Seeing that I had caught up, Larry asked, "Did you see anything you wanted in there Jay?"

I turned away quickly so he wouldn't see my face. Shaking my head, I said, "No."

Of all my friends, Larry was the only one who really cared. He seemed to understand how I felt and he did his best to support me. But with Billy and Lonnie there, I couldn't look him in the eye or even attempt to put my feelings into words. It would have been too hard.

Billy picked up a rock and threw it at the horse. He missed, but the horse jumped back and trotted out to pasture.

Lonnie gave Billy a dirty look. "Don't do that. It's taken me months to get that horse to come to me, and you're going to spoil it all by being mean!"

Billy just laughed and getting back on his bike, he spun the back tire spitting rocks and dirt everywhere as he took off.

We left Main Street and rode down the Bangerter trail. Passing our little neighborhood we continued on toward the old swimming hole. This would be our first swim of the summer. The sun was high in the sky and with very little breeze we soon worked up a sweat.

In spite of the heat, my friends were gaining speed. I knew better but I pushed down hard on the pedals trying to keep up and the chain on my bike sprung off. It caught on the back fender and wrapped around the sprocket. Immediately, the back wheel seized up and sent me flying over the handlebars head first. I reached out my hands and hit the ground.

Landing hard, the air was completely knocked from my lungs. I skidded on my hands and chin until I came to a stop. Gasping for air, I tried to sit up but could only roll onto my back until I could take more than tiny gasps. Finally able to breathe, I waited for the stars to disappear from around my head and then I looked back. My bike was lying on top of me. The leg of my coveralls had caught in the chain.

I tried to kick the bike away from me. "You stupid bike! What a piece of junk," I yelled trying to hold back the tears. I gave my bike another push. This time my pant leg gave way and *The Monster* slid back. I looked down at my hands. Both palms were bloody. I reached up to feel my chin and blood dripped on my hand. I gave my bike another hard kick and screamed at it again but I only succeeded in hurting my foot. As I recoiled in pain, I wondered if *The Monster* was paying me back for all the bad things I said about it over the years.

As much as I was trying to hold back my tears, the tears of my friends were freely flowing—but not because they felt sorry for me. They were laughing so hard they were crying. Billy fell off his bike holding his side. He laughed for several minutes before he stood up again. Billy always enjoyed everyone else's pain and this was the second time in two days he had found the chance to laugh at me.

"This stinks," I said as I picked up my piece of junk. Putting down the kick stand I surveyed the situation. The chain was tangled around the back sprocket and it was caught in the brake. It wouldn't move. It was jammed so tightly that I would have to take the back tire off and undo the chain to get it back together. I sent it flying off the trail into the ditch with another kick from my aching foot. It tumbled over once—then came to a stop against a fence post.

Being careful to not hurt my hands, I dusted off my coveralls and began to pick up my candy, which was spread out all over the trail. On my hands and knees I carefully salvaged each piece dusting it off on my shirt before I put it back in the bag. The stinging in my hands and chin was starting to build. I needed to clean the scratches out in the worst way. I could feel little pieces of rock under my skin.

Larry pulled his bike up next to me. "Come and sit on the handlebars and I'll give you a ride to the pond. You can wash off once we get there."

Waiting for no one, Billy was already on his way. Lonnie rode next to us as Larry pumped hard weaving back and forth across the trail fighting to keep from falling over with me on the handlebars. Finally we both got the hang of it and began to gain speed.

The tall weeds along the train trail blurred past and when we reached the turnoff to the pond, Larry slowed down to let me jump off. He walked his bike alongside me as we made our way down the last part of the trail to the pond. I wiped my chin on my shirt to see how much blood there was and found that it had dried.

When we arrived, Billy was already there and Lonnie was pulling his bike up to the big cottonwood tree that hung out in all directions over the pond. Above us a big black crow circled the pond letting out a screech of protest at our invasion of its sacred ground. Insects skittered over the pond and butterflies danced through the willows. The weeds were already getting high and the narrow pathway to the pond was slick with mud. A thick layer of clover covered the ground underneath the cottonwood tree. It was soft and cool under our feet—the perfect place to spend hours on end.

How long the old cottonwood tree had been there no one knew but it was so big around that all three of us could hide on one side and not be seen from the trail. Long before us, someone had nailed old pieces of wood up the side of the tree to the largest branch that hung out over the pond. The huge limb was wide enough to provide a walkway out to where an old rope hung from a higher branch. We had tied a smaller rope to the large one so that we could pull the big rope in and swing out over the water.

Scrambling out of my coveralls and boots, I hung my clothes on an old rusty nail sticking from the tree. Forgetting about my scraped hands and chin, I ran down to the edge of the pond and jumped into the air. Tucking my legs up and wrapping my arms around them, I splashed into the water. The shock of the cold water reached all my muscles at the same instant making me gasp as I kicked to the surface.

"YAHOO, that's cold," I screamed, swimming quickly to shore.

The guys were laughing and screaming at me when I got out shivering. Billy was climbing up the side of the tree while Lonnie folded his clothes, stacking them in a pile by the roots of the tree. Larry had one shoe off and was working on a knot in the other shoe, trying to hurry. His pants were bundled up around his knees.

Larry finally got his shoe untied and slipped it off along with his pants. Hanging them over a small branch he stepped through the clover toward the ladder going up the side of the tree. Billy had reached the end of the branch. He was 20 feet in the air, leaning over to grab the rope that was tied to the rope swing. Pulling it toward him he wrapped his fingers around it.

"Watch this you guys, I'm going to do a big dive."

He pushed off swinging down and out over the water. A large knot tied at the bottom was just right to support his feet as he swung out over the pond. When the rope had reached the end of its arc, Billy pushed off with his feet and letting go at the same time, he flew through the air arching his back. His hands reached out towards the water as his body went straight in with a big splash.

Seconds later his head burst out of the cold water. Gasping for air, he yelled, "Holy cow that's cold." He kicked hard and with arms flaying wildly, he swam to shore. He pulled himself out onto the clover searching for a patch of sun.

When it was my turn, I climbed the steps up the tree. Reaching the large branch I steadied myself scrapping the mud from my feet. I grabbed the rope with both hands, then I swung out over the water. But when I kicked and let go to execute my dive, my foot caught in the rope and I ended up hitting the water flat on my back. For the second time today I had the air knocked out of me. The cold water cut into every nerve and I struggled to stay afloat while I caught my breath. I found myself making tiny gasping noises as I tried to get the air to enter my lungs. In the midst of my struggle, I felt a strong arm around my shoulder and a calm voice telling me to relax—that I was okay.

It seemed like forever but when I could finally breathe, Billy turned me loose and we both paddled back to the edge of the pond. Billy didn't say a word. I wondered if my keeping silent the night before had anything to do with his silence now. Regardless, I was grateful—more than words could tell. We both pulled ourselves through the mud and onto the clover. I pulled my feet up under me and tried to slow my breathing. At the same time I tried to hold the heat inside as the warm sun beat down on my back. We watched as Larry and Lonnie both took a turn. Splash! ...Splash!

We swam and sat in the sun and ate candy from our bags until the sun sent streaks of red through the wispy clouds near the horizon. It had been such a perfect afternoon that I had almost forgotten what lay ahead for me. I was on foot and my bike was still in the ditch.

We gathered our clothes and got dressed; then traversed the muddy path that lead back to the old Bangerter trail. My friends walked their bikes alongside me 'til we arrived where I had left *The Monster*. It really looked like a monster too—all tangled up in itself. As much as I wanted to walk away and leave it there to rot in the ditch, I knew I needed a bike. Reluctantly, I drug it out of the weeds and picked up the back tire. Pushing it on the front tire I began the long walk home.

My friends rode slowly alongside me for a while but it was getting darker by the minute. Eventually, they said goodbye and left me by myself pushing my piece of junk. The shadows were rapidly replacing the streaks of red on the horizon. The trail that I knew like the back of my hand in the daylight was scary in the dark.

I turned my thoughts toward a new bike to keep the darkness from enveloping me.

I wanted a bike so badly it made my hands sweat. Riding by the bike shop earlier had made my insides hurt—especially watching someone else get a new bike. Having a new bike was all I could think about when I was awake. When I slept I dreamed the same dream, over and over again: *floating across town on a new bike—envious friends begging me for a chance to ride my bike.*

I knew that there was no chance for a dream like that to come true. It was ridiculous. Every once in a while I had taken the subject up with my parents but I always got the same answer: "Sorry, Jay. We just don't have the money now. Maybe next Christmas."

It was so late when I got home that I secretly wondered if seeing my busted bike would change my parent's minds about a new bike. It didn't.

Chapter 6
The Big Red Bike

I woke up the following Saturday chomping at the bit to start the day. On the refrigerator I found my weekly "To Do" list which I looked over quickly and placed on the table. After a quick breakfast, I headed out the door with my baseball glove in hand.

Larry showed up late for our game. He had forgotten his glove and none of us could find a baseball anyway. For some reason, baseballs were always disappearing. Everyone blamed it on the dogs in the neighborhood, but if we didn't put them away, we could never find them again.

We pulled out the football and got another game going. The neighbors from across the street joined us. Larry, Lonnie, Billy and I were on one team. Jody, his brother, Mark and the Jones boys lined up against us.

Not too far into the game, I hiked the ball to Larry. He handed off to Billy who flew around the corner with his arm outstretched to keep Jody away. Jody (a year younger than I) came naively ahead for the tackle. His nose and Billy's hand made hard contact and it was Jody that went down—blood gushing everywhere. He rolled over holding his nose, tears streaming down his cheeks. He struggled to sit up while his brother Mark hurried over to help. Seeing all the blood, Mark turned to Billy.

"Oh, is my dad going to be mad at you!"

Billy got that *don't mess with me* look on his face. Jody got up with both hands covering his nose.

Blood running between his fingers and down his shirt he took off for home. Mark followed.

Their dad was known for his hot temper and nobody wanted to be around when the news got to him. Billy looked around and said, "Game's over. It's *hunt and run fun time*. Let's get out of here."

My friends ran for the corner of the house where they had left their bikes. I opened the door, threw the ball inside and yelled to my sister that I was leaving. We were gone in 30 seconds. Each of us shot down the street to our designated collection routes.

In less than an hour we were at Larry's with a load of bottles ready to make the run to Dansie's Market. While my friends wrapped the bottles in newspaper to protect them for the trip, I tightened the chain on my bike. The trip took about 20 minutes—for my friends. It took a lot longer for me. It was hard to trust my old rusty bike after my last accident and I was traveling a lot slower these days. I wasn't taking any chances. It had taken me a long time to get the back tire off and the chain untangled after my last accident on the way to the swimming hole. It would take me a lot longer to live down the humiliation.

When I made the turn onto Main Street, my friends were way ahead of me. I approached the bicycle shop and decided to stop. If I had been with my friends they would have been impatient and I wouldn't have been able to really look. But I was alone and I was going to take my time. They couldn't "cash in" without me anyway. I had a lot of the bottles in my basket. They would have to wait.

What I saw made my heart come to a complete stop. Positioned in the front window on a stand that made it clearly visible from the street was the most beautiful site my eyes had ever seen. I didn't inhale again until I had carefully taken in the whole thing—from one glistening fender to the other. My mouth lay wide open for the longest time as I stared in awe.

The sun was shining in the window and it caught the chrome fenders at just the right angle to send light in every direction. It was dazzling. The frame was bright red with a large red and white seat that had big chrome springs underneath it.

The bike was obviously designed for comfort. Most impressive to me was the red and chrome tank between the top bar and the second bar with the words SCHWINN scrolled across it. Across the red chain guard was the word, JAGUAR.

I don't remember how long I stood there in the sun gazing through the window until I realized that sweat was rolling off the end of my nose and that the front of my shirt was soaking wet. I pushed my bike around the corner and leaned it against the side of the building in the shade. Then, wiping the sweat from my forehead I tucked my baseball hat into my back pocket and walked to the front door.

I pushed on the door but it wouldn't budge. I pushed harder and felt a cool breeze pushing back at me from the other side of the door. Pressing harder, the door gave way and I stepped into bicycle heaven. I worked my way past the row of new bikes until I arrived at the front window.

There it was, sitting on its throne crowned with a large, chrome carrying bracket on the front and a chrome headlight mounted in the center of the handlebars. Between the top bar and the second bar, holding the front and back wheels in line was the amazing tank. It looked like a fancy gas tank. The bike was incredible and the longer I looked at it the more I noticed. There was a shiny red passenger seat behind the red and white driver's seat and underneath the back seat was a tail light. I reached down and flipped the switch; the tail light turned on brightly. In amazement, I turned off the light and let my gaze wander to something I had never seen before on a bike. I stepped up onto the front window display and reached across the handlebars to a small box with a lever and the numbers 1, 2, and 3 written on it. I flipped the lever back and forth. I was so engrossed that I didn't hear anyone come up behind me.

"We just got it in here yesterday." said a voice from behind me. "I couldn't wait to get it in the window for everyone to see." I turned around with a start and jumped back knocking the bike toward the window. Mr. Paterson reached over me and grabbed the seat in time to keep the bike from falling over.

A bit embarrassed, I smiled and said, "I have never seen anything like it before."

"I was reluctant to bring this bike in," said Mr. Paterson. "I didn't know if anyone around here could afford a fancy bike like this."

I had looked at every bike that had come and gone in the shop for the past several months since the store had opened. This was the brightest paint job I had ever seen and it was polished to such a shine that I could see the reflection of passing cars in it. Every bolt was buffed to perfection. The brake controls were mounted on the handlebars both left and right. Next to the right handle grip was the chrome box with the lever to work the 3-speed control. I followed the grey rubber-covered cable from the speed control until it disappeared inside the tank and down to the rear hub. There was a small button on the side of the tank. I reached over and pushed it with my finger. A horn sounded with a smart beep.

"It has a horn too! Wow," I said.

This bike had everything! Something inside me was about to explode. My insides felt like a giant storm building pressure and about to release a torrent. My fingers were twitching and my feet would not hold still. Mr. Paterson watched me go over every inch of the bike. Every time I touched something he was right there with his red grease rag.

Reaching over my shoulder to wipe my fingerprints off the handlebars, he said, "Well? How do you like the new Mark II Jaguar, Jay?"

"Wow, three speeds; how did they do that?"

I followed the cable with my finger along the new brake system. He reached over and wiped my prints off. He spent the next few minutes showing me how it worked and how to adjust everything.

When I asked him how much it cost, he smiled and said, "$129.95 with everything you see here." With a chuckle in his voice he asked, "When do you want to pick it up?"

I almost fell off the window display when I heard the price. "That's a whole lot of money," I said. I stepped back to get the full view. That bike looked like it could fly.

Mr. Paterson reached over and pushed the button again on the side of the tank. It let out a sharp beep. "That beep sounds like your beep to me," he said.

I frowned as my shoulders slumped and my eyes fell from the bike to the floor. "I could never own a bike like this, Mr. Paterson; only in my dreams."

Mr. Paterson reached over and ruffled my hair. He paused and then looked me straight in the eyes. In a caring voice he said, "Jay, you can do anything you want in this world. Never give up on your dreams because dreams come true for those who work hard and believe."

They do? I thought. For the first time in my life I considered the possibility. In that same moment I decided I was going to have that bike. I had no idea how, but I knew that the bike in the window was meant to me mine! I just had to figure out a way to earn the money before someone else bought it.

Looking at Mr. Paterson I smiled and with a slow retreat I stepped back away from the Big Red Bike. "I gotta get goin' right now Mr. Paterson, I told him. "I sure wish that bike could be mine."

"Don't give up, Jay," he said as he turned around waving the red rag over his shoulder.

"Goodbye," I said in a barely audible whisper, my eyes still scanning the incredible red bike as I left.

I let out a huge sigh as I rounded the corner. Getting back on the old green monster was very hard to do. I couldn't quit staring at the bike in the window as I peddled past the shop. Pushing the rusty pedals toward Dansie's Market was harder than ever. I had to completely reset my focus to even think about meeting up with my friends. I knew they would be anxious and maybe even mad at me for taking so long. I found them sitting outside Dansie's, waiting.

"We thought you'd had another accident and couldn't get that piece of crap going again," Billy laughed.

Larry got to his feet and immediately inspected the pop bottles to make sure they weren't broken. "You stopped at the bike shop didn't you?" he asked. "I can always tell because you have that far away look in your eyes. You're dreaming again, Jay!"

It was true. I was dreaming. When I closed my eyes all I could see was the Big Red Bike sitting in the bicycle shop window. What was wrong with dreaming anyway? Just like Mr. Paterson had said, *"...never give up on your dreams."* I realized as I thought about it that without a dream a person didn't have anything to live for—and my dream was certainly something to live for! My dream was beginning to build inside me. Somehow I was going to have that bike.

With a scowl on my face and a flicker of anger in my voice, I gave Billy a shove and said, "Stop buggin' me about the bike!"

He grabbed my shirt and almost lifted me off the ground. Pushing me back against Dansie's window, he growled in a low menacing voice, "Don't go pushin' me, Jay. You hear me?!" The anger in his eyes left me cold and scared.

He let go of me brushing his hands across my chest like he was wiping his hand prints off my shirt. I looked into his eyes. They were filled with that, *"I will break your face"* look. Knowing I had gone too far, I waved him away as I turned around and walked inside. I found a cart and pushed it back out to load the bottles.

Mr. Dansie was sweeping the store when we pushed the cart back inside. He greeted us as always and went to the counter to tally up the value of our bottles. We collected our weekly fill of candy and headed for home. Billy didn't say another word and took off ahead of us.

It was a hard ride home. I was still angry at Billy but more than that I had seen the bike of my dreams. All I could think about was the Big Red Bike shimmering in the bike shop window. Every time I moved the slightest bit in my seat, it would twist to one side. I was so fed up with my old piece of junk that I envisioned myself throwing it in the swimming hole. Nothing would make me happier than to finally be rid of it—especially if I could ride away on the Big Red Bike.

Chapter 7
The Big Boss

Once at home, I found myself sitting under the peach tree in the back yard. With pencil and paper in hand, I began to write down every idea that came into my mind.

How does a 9-year-old boy earn $130.00? I asked myself. *I'm just a kid with a big dream.* It was one thing to hold onto your dreams like Mr. Paterson had said, but, *How did you make your dreams come true?* I wondered.

That night after dinner we sat in the living room listening to the radio. My folks were bent over it like they could see the person talking. It was the first time I can remember that I never heard a word. Finally, I stood up, said good night, and went to my bedroom. Lying on my bed looking at the light in the middle of the ceiling, my thoughts were still on just one thing. I went to sleep and dreamed the same dream—only this time I wasn't riding just any new bike, I was riding **The Big Red Bike.**

For the next week I couldn't think about anything else. I had yard work to do—and plenty of time to dream. But I still didn't know how I was going to earn the money to buy the Big Red Bike. Sometimes I let myself get discouraged.

Who am I fooling anyway? You can buy a candy bar for a nickel and you can go to the movies for a dime. Where am I going to get $130.00? I asked myself.

But deep inside I knew I could find a way. Several times a day I added to the list of things I thought I might be able to do to earn money.

I have two lawn-mowing jobs now, I thought to myself. *They're good for $1.00 every week. I can always pull weeds for extra change.* But that came to a grand total of 12—maybe 15 dollars for the whole summer. After that I had no idea what to do.

It was time to find help. It was Saturday morning and my dad was working in the garage making a small cabinet out of scrap wood. It was the one thing he loved to do and it brought in some extra money. I sat down on the bench next to him and poured out my heart in one long sentence.

"I saw a new bike I want to buy—I know you can't help—but I want to earn the money and I don't know what to do—I can mow lawns and do stuff like that but I know I just want that bike."

Dad stopped what he was doing and turned toward me. Looking down through his glasses, he said, "That's a big problem for such a young man, Jay. Do you think you can find enough lawns to mow to save that kind of money?"

I shook my head back and forth, "No, not in this neighborhood." I went on. "There are only about eight, maybe ten people in the whole neighborhood who would be the least bit interested in letting me cut their grass. At $1.00 a week that's only $40.00 a month—*if* I could find 10 people—less the gas I would have to buy," I said.

Dad leaned over to pick up the hand saw. Sitting up, he cut off a small piece of wood with a quick draw on the saw. "The only answer I can give you is to get out there and see what you can find. And don't forget that you can always ask for help from someone who knows everything." He paused and putting the saw down, he turned back to me. "When I was in 8th grade, my mom needed help and extra money. I had to quit school to keep my mom and me alive. She told me the same thing I just told you. She sent me to the bedroom and told me to take it up with the 'Big Boss'." Dad bowed his head and got real quiet for a minute. He folded his hands over his knees and turned around to face me again. "Have you done that yet? Sometimes He will lead us where we need to go."

That was one thing I understood. My mom had come into my bedroom every night for as long as I could remember and asked, "Did you say your prayers, Jay?" I felt good when I prayed, but it was always the same kind of a prayer. *Bless my family;*

keep me safe; tell my sister to be nice to me; and always keep mean Billy as my friend.

That night I laid in bed after mom had tucked me in. There wasn't anyone who could help me figure this problem out except maybe the "Big Boss." I slipped out of bed landing on my knees. I folded my hands together and for the first time in my life, I *really* prayed.

After begging for help and ideas, I thanked Him for everything else, just like I always did. Then I crawled back under the covers.

My eyes were wide open and couldn't find a way to get to sleep. I could see the bright full moon through my window reflecting off the big leaves of the maple tree. My mind kept taking me back to the window in the bike shop. All I could see was the Big Red Bike. I tossed and turned watching the moon crawl through the maple tree one inch at a time until it faded from sight. It seemed like hours before I drifted off to sleep. Then I had one dream after another. Each one ended the same way—with me riding down the street on the new, Red, Jaguar Schwinn 3-speed.

The next week things started to happen. My neighbor Mark had been delivering door hangers every other morning for a local business. He got paid a penny a house. When Mark got a new job bagging groceries at Dansie's, he turned over his old job to his brother, Jody. The only problem was that the job began at 5:30 in the morning and Jody couldn't get out of bed on time. Mark was having a conversation with his old boss when I went out to start looking for lawn mowing jobs. He saw me and waved for me to come over.

I looked at him and mouthed, "Do you want me?"

He waved again so I approached them. The man turned around and looked at me, sizing me up.

"Morning Jay," said Mark, "This here is my old boss, Mr. Jepson. He's got a job if you're interested—three mornings a week. Do you like to run?"

I had no idea what I was getting myself into but when he said "*job*" I knew it was for me!

I said, "I love to run. How much can I make?"

The man explained that he worked for an advertising company. He had a route to work each week—Monday, Wednesday, and Friday. He would pay cash at the end of every day. He said he had two other boys who worked with him and that he would pick me up at 5:30 in the morning. If I could keep up, I could have the job. Mark said I could earn about $1.50 a day. Every penny I earned would put me closer to my goal.

Elated, I headed down the street to see if I could find anyone interested in letting me cut their lawn. I visited every home trying to sell them on the fact that I could do a better job than they could. After a long morning of door knocking I had lined up two new jobs.

The widow Sorenson lived around the corner and down the street. She wanted me to mow the lawn and to help her with all the weeds each week. I figured that would bring in a little extra. Then there was Mr. Henderson and his wife. She worked at the military base like so many others. She hated doing the yard work and he was a big man who couldn't get around very well. Their two kids were grown up and gone so it was an easy sell. He was really glad to see me when he found out what I was there for. I made appointments to cut both lawns.

One thing became clear to me. My summer of fun with friends was about to end. If I spent the summer working for this bike there would be no time for swimming at the pond, no more *hunt and run fun* days, and no hard-fought football games in the front yard. Those were sad thoughts for a 9-year-old boy but if that's what it was going to take, then that's what I was willing to give up. There were only 12 weeks left before school and I had a lot of money to earn.

I decided it was time to fix up my old bike. Every time I went anywhere I was taking my life in my hands. Besides, I was going to need it to help me earn the money for my new bike. I went into the garage and took apart *The Monster*. I cut off the old sticky electrical tape on the handlebars and replaced it. I put bolts and screws where bailing wire had been. I worked on the fenders and hammered out some of the worst dents. I took a small pair of pliers and adjusted the spokes until the rims started to look the way they were meant to look. When I was finished, the tires didn't even rub on the fenders anymore. I stood back and took a look. It would have to last me just a little while longer.

Chapter 8
Hot to Trot

I already missed my friends. They had come by in the morning to go frog hunting but I had plans to scour the neighborhood for more lawn mowing jobs. Now, at the end of the day I decided to check in with them and see what was going on. I picked up my newly refurbished bike and headed to Lonnie's.

As I pulled up I could see lights flooding the driveway. The garage door was open and on the workbench was the go-cart. Everyone was around it. Just as I poked my head in the garage door Lonnie pulled the starter rope. The engine sputtered and a puff of smoke shot in his face. Then it quit. Lonnie waved his hand to clear the smoke as his dad pulled the rope again, giving it a mighty jerk. It sputtered, but this time it caught on as his dad pushed the choke in. Rough at first, the engine soon smoothed out. Lonnie reached over to a lever next to the floor in front of the seat. Pulling it back, the engine got louder. After a minute, Lonnie's dad reached over and pushed a piece of metal over on top of the spark plug and the engine stopped.

I walked into the garage. It smelled of gas and oil. Larry was the first to see me. He grabbed my coat. "You're just in time, Jay. We're about to see if this thing will really work!"

"Each one of you grab one of the wheels and let's lift it to the ground," Lonnie's dad said as he looked the four of us over.

I moved to one of the back wheels and the others each grabbed a wheel. We lifted it off the workbench and set it on the ground. I grabbed hold of the steering wheel and gave it a turn. The front wheels moved easily left and right. The excitement was building. Billy and Lonnie were pushing for the chance to be the first one to drive it down the driveway.

Lonnie's dad settled that as fast as it started. "Lonnie, since this is yours, climb in and give it a try."

A broad smile swept over Lonnie's face as he gently nudged Billy aside. Slipping his legs down under the wheel he was ready. A large pedal was located by his right foot.

"That's the brake, Lonnie," said his father. "Just push it to slow down, but make sure you pull back on the gas, okay?"

Lonnie nodded his head and Larry grabbed the starter rope, pulling hard. The engine jumped to life. On the left side was the lever that released the wheels. Lonnie reached over and slowly pulled it back. The cart started to move and he turned it sharply around heading down the driveway. He gave it a little more gas. The engine roared louder as it jumped and picked up speed—a little too much speed. Lonnie jerked the wheel back and forth trying to put his foot on the brake and pull back the gas at the same time. We all laughed when his dad had to go running down the driveway to catch him before he went into the street. Before the night was over we all had the chance to take the go-cart up and down the driveway.

The late night air was chilly when we pulled down the garage door and turned out the lights. We headed off to our homes with the smell of exhaust in our hair and gas on our hands.

The next morning came early. For the first time in my life that didn't require a fishing pole, I was up before 5:30. I managed to grab a glass of milk and one of mom's homemade rolls. The light was just creeping over the Rocky Mountains pushing back the early morning darkness when I sat down on the front steps to wait for Mr. Jepson. The morning dew glistened on the tips of the grass and the street light down the road flickered, trying to decide whether to be on or off. A dog barked down the street and as I lifted my eyes, I heard the sound of a truck coming around the corner. I glanced through the window at the clock on the wall; it was 5:30—right on time.

Without a word, Mr. Jepson waved for me to get in the back of the truck. I jumped in and we headed out. There were two other guys in the truck. They were older than I was and they acted like I wasn't there. We drove to a neighborhood on the other end of town. The homes were old army twin homes. The breeze was chilly that early in the morning riding in the back of the truck and I was glad when we finally stopped.

Mr. Jepson stepped out holding a clipboard. "Jay, this is Mike and Jerry." I nodded at them and they did the same. "Let's get started. Mike you take that side of the street and Jerry you take the other." He reached in the back of the truck and picked up two bundles of plastic bags. Handing one to each fellow, he wrote down the number of bags on his paper as they each started down the street.

"Jump in, Jay I'm taking you to the other end." Stepping back up into the truck he drove down the street around the corner and to the other end of the block. He handed me two bundles. "Okay, start down this street on one side, then cross the street and go down the other side. Wait here when you're done. I'll pick you up." Without another word he started up the truck and was gone.

The sun was now peeking over the tops of the mountains filling the sky with a dim light that warmed my face. A red robin hopped across the grass looking for a morning breakfast of worms. I remembered what Mr. Jepson had said: *If you can keep up, you can have the job.* I began running from one door to the next dropping one bag of papers on each porch.

One house after another; one street after another. After the first hour, every house looked the same. My side began to ache and my feet got heavier with every doorstep. The sweat rolled off my nose and down my back. Each breath hurt my lungs. I wasn't sure I had made the right decision in accepting this job.

Just as I crossed the street to work my way down the other side, a big black dog came charging around the corner. He stopped and sized me up as I did the same. A slow growl made me ask myself, *Is getting this packet on the porch worth a penny or should I get away while I can?* I decided to take my chances but as soon as I made a move in the direction of the house the dog bolted toward me—teeth bared and growling. I had no idea what to do and as the dog got closer, I dropped on my backside so that I could use my feet to fend off the dog if I needed to. At the same time, I figured I could crawl backward and try to get away.

The big dog arrived but instead of attacking, he put his huge paws on my chest and with slobber dripping from his mouth he started at my chin and ran his tongue all the way up to the top of my head—again and again. I thought I was going to suffocate when finally a small lady in a long green robe pushed the screen door open. "Back off Maggie," she scolded. The dog jumped to attention and ran to the woman on the porch. "Sorry boy," she said. "She's just a loving puppy. Are you okay?"

I scrambled to my feet and dropping a packet on the sidewalk I tried to smile as I wiped the slobber from my face. I was so shook up I couldn't get out an answer to the woman's question, but I was happy to find a sprinkler watering the grass several houses down the street. I just stood in it for the longest time, washing my face and breathing hard.

The next street was the hardest of all. With wet clothes and soggy feet, I didn't think I would make it to the end. I stopped and closed my eyes. I let the vision of the Big Red Bike fill my mind. I could see it sitting in the window; then I saw myself riding it down the street and I knew I had to keep going. As my clothes dried out and as the heat from my body dried my shoes I felt myself getting a second wind.

Three hours later, Mr. Jepson dropped me off at my house. I crawled out of the truck and landed on the ground. My legs were weak and I fell to my knees. I wasn't sure I would ever walk again. Sitting in the truck on the way home, the strength had left my legs and it was all I could do to keep from throwing up. I felt the color drain from my face. I bent over and gagged but there was nothing there so I put my head between my knees and took a few deep, long breaths.

Mr. Jepson shut off the old 1944 Ford pickup truck and a loud BANG exploded out the exhaust pipe—along with a puff of black smoke. I heard the truck door open and the rustle of papers as he slid out the seat. I watched his feet hit the ground and I sat up trying not to let him know I felt like a dog wanting to puke. He reached back inside and brought out a large leather folder with a clipboard and pencil. He paid the older boys first, then sat down next to me on the grass.

"You did all right today, Jay. Not bad for your first day." Picking up his pencil and checking his notes he figured out how many bags I had delivered—153. He handed me $1.53.

I said goodbye to Mr. Jepson and the other boys as they pulled away. I struggled to my feet and headed toward the house. If I hadn't wanted that bike so badly I know I never would have delivered for him again. But I was on my way to earning that beautiful red bike and I was willing to do whatever it took.

I passed through the kitchen on the way to get a hot shower. There was freshly baked bread sitting on the counter. Without a thought I opened the knife drawer and picked out a sharp knife. Then with one smooth cut I sliced the end off a new loaf of bread. I reached inside and ripped the middle of the loaf out leaving the hard outside crust. I squeezed it together in my hand and took a big bite. There was nothing in the world like my mom's homemade bread. I replaced the end and put the loaf up against the back of the counter— maybe I would get away with it. Then I staggered into the bathroom for a long, hot shower.

I did some quick figuring while the water ran over my head. If I could find more lawn mowing jobs and keep this job, I could earn about $9.50 a week. That was $38.00 a month—not enough. I turned off the shower, dried off, picked up my clothes, and put them in the hamper. I wrapped the towel around me and headed for my bedroom for a nap. Getting up at 5:30 would take some getting used to.

While I slept I had another dream. This time I was floating in slow motion trying to drop bags of papers on porches. Every time I got close to the porch it would move away. *How would I ever earn the money for my bike if I couldn't get the papers on the porch?* When I woke up, I was soaked with sweat. The dream was a little too real and it reminded me of how close I was to the Big Red Bike – yet still so far away.

My sister had gone to work. I was alone in the house. I got dressed and pulled on my boots. I went to open the front door to let in the sun but my legs were stiff and sore. I could hardly take the steps down to the yard. I sat down on the porch with my elbows pressed against the step behind me. My neck was sore too. I leaned my head back working my neck back and forth to loosen the muscles.

After a few minutes of stretching, my body would finally move. I got on my bike to see what was happening with the go-cart before I mowed Mr. Henderson's lawn. I peddled slowly to Lonnie's house. My legs felt like jelly and they screamed with each push of the pedal. I pulled slowly into the front yard and laid the bike down on the grass. I could hear the guys laughing on the other side of the house. They were all crowded around the go-cart. Lonnie was attaching something to the back of the frame. They turned around as I walked up and I could see the small plaque hanging from the back. Red with white letters spelled out, "HOT TO TROT."

"It's ready to go," said Larry. "We get to take it out for the first time tomorrow."

Lonnie's dad opened the door to the house and leaned out, "Anyone for peanut butter and jam sams?"

It didn't take any of us more than a few seconds to push through the door and into the kitchen.

"Here are the rules," his father explained while we poured milk into our glasses. "First, no one drives this on the road. You'll have to pull it over to the school parking lot before you start it. And never ...and I mean NEVER run it on the roads. Do you guys understand?"

With a sandwich in one hand and a glass of milk in the other, we all nodded in agreement.

"Can we take it to the school tomorrow sometime?" asked Lonnie.

"Yes, but follow the rules." Lonnie's dad turned and left the room, while we planned the next day.

"I have to work most of the day," I said.

They didn't really hear me, nor did they care what I said. Their minds were intent on taking the go-cart out in the school parking lot. When we had finished, we put our glasses in the sink and agreed to meet around noon. Everyone headed home.

It was just after 8:00 a.m. the next morning when I pushed the lawn mower out of the garage. I had to be done with my lawn jobs before I met my friends at noon. I had checked the gas and oil just like my dad taught me and I had topped off the small gas tank from the extra gallon of gas we kept for the mower. Just as I arrived at the widow's house Phil Fox, the paperboy came riding toward me.

He stopped and asked, "Can I talk with you for a minute?"

I had never spoken to Phil before. He was four years older than I was and I wondered what he wanted. I stopped pushing the mower and looked way up into his narrow face. He was really tall. He had bright red hair that was combed from both sides into the center with a curly lock that fell down the middle of his forehead, and a full face of freckles. His white T-shirt sleeves were rolled up two or three times.

Slowly, he began. "My mom and dad are fixin' to move to Ogden this next weekend and I need to find someone to take over the paper route before I leave. Are you interested in a good job earning about 20 bucks a month?" He reached into his back pocket and pulled out a black comb. He combed his hair back over the top and reached up with his finger to pull the hair down in the middle of his forehead.

"Are you kidding? Sure I am," I said.

He climbed off his bike and sat down on the grass. I sat down next to him while he explained to me all about the job. He wanted to make sure he got paid for the papers he had delivered so we figured it all out. I was going to take over the route the following Saturday—the day he moved.

It was starting to amaze me. Just a few days ago I had made a decision to earn the Big Red Bike. Today I could see it was possible. I could see a light at the end of the tunnel and it was getting brighter each day.

I got to my feet and said, "Thanks, man. This is so great, I really needed this job." He smiled and without a word he climbed on his bike and headed down the road.

Leaning over the lawn mower, I pulled the starter rope as hard as I could. Smoke blasted from the exhaust. Back and forth across the grass I went with the mower. Every time the bag filled up with clippings I shut the mower off, unhooked the bag and carried it to the garbage can. Soon, I figured out that the garbage can wasn't going to hold all the grass clippings. I would need to figure out another way to get rid of the grass.

I ran home and pulled a large piece of canvas out of the garage and took it back with me. I laid it out on the driveway and piled the grass on it. After finishing the job, I folded the corners up and drug it to the end of the street. There was a field with a few horses in it. I dumped the grass over the fence, folded the canvas and ran back to the widow's house. She was waiting on the porch for me with a glass of pink lemonade in her hand.

The next thing I knew I was weeding around the house while she sat in a lawn chair telling me about her late husband—how she loved him and how good he was to her, how he had died three years earlier. I also learned about *all* their children *and* grandchildren *and* just about everything there was to know about her dog. At last, the weeds were gone. I had consumed about a gallon of lemonade. She paid me and I headed for home with sweat rolling down my back and my hands caked with dried mud.

On the way, I passed Mr. Gerber sitting on his porch with his push mower in the driveway. I recognized another opportunity.

"Hi Mr. Gerber," I began. "Can I cut your grass for you? It'll only cost you a dollar to cut the front and back yard."

He stood up and walked over to me, putting his hand on my shoulder. "How about right now, Jay? I don't think I can push that mower over there one more foot."

I still had time before I had to meet my friends. I reached down and pulled the starting rope. On the third pull the mover puffed to life and started to purr. It only took me a little over an hour. He was still sitting on the front porch sipping a Coke when I pushed the mower through the gate into the front yard. He reached into his pocket and handed me a one dollar bill along with an extra 25 cents. I set my next appointment for the following week.

I wasn't far from home. I hurried to put the mower away. I ran into the house and found my sister sitting at the table with a bowl of beans and ham and a slice of homemade bread sitting on the table.

"Sit down, Jay. It's time you had some lunch."

Three minutes later my plate was clean. I grabbed my baseball cap and flew out the door. I arrived a little after noon. Larry was tying the cart to the back of Billy's bike. Lonnie was sitting in the cart to guide it. I dropped my bike and positioned myself next to Larry to help push from behind. We started down the road toward the big school parking lot. We had to follow the road and it was about a half mile.

We pushed and pulled the cart into the lot and untied it with a fury. Lonnie was still sitting in the seat and Larry gave the rope a pull. The motor sputtered to life on the first pull. Lonnie pushed the throttle forward and with his other hand pulled the lever that released the wheels. The cart took off with a jerk and within seconds it was speeding around the parking lot. We took turns racing it around and around. It was the first time any of us had ever driven a real powered *anything.* We felt all grown up—like we were racing a real racecar around the track. We decided to bring a watch next time and to set up a small track to see who could run it the fastest.

We ran out of gas after about two hours. We pulled and pushed the cart back to the neighborhood and into Lonnie's garage. I invited everyone over for a backyard sleepover after dinner. They all agreed to come.

Chapter 9
Summer Fun

We rolled out our sleeping bags underneath the peach tree in the backyard. Then we waited until the lights went out. When my dad finally turned off the last light we all jumped over the fence. Our bikes were under the maple tree all lined up and ready to go. We pushed them quietly out the yard and headed for the Davis Drive-in Theatre.

I had a flashlight taped to my handlebars so we could see as we rode down the Bangerter trail. We arrived along the edge of the pond and stashed our bikes under the trees. Then we followed the ditch until it came to the back of the drive-in. There, we crawled under the fence and entered the theater.

Most of the cars were several rows ahead of us. The ones on the back row had guys with their girlfriends. The windows were always so fogged they couldn't have seen us if they had tried. (It was years before I figured out why the windows were foggy.)

This was a movie everyone had been waiting for. It was called *Footsteps in the Sand* with Stewart Granger and Jean Simmons. We were laughing most of the time—climbing up the trees and running around—we never really figured out the plot of the movie. My sister told mom the next day that it was a love story with a lot of deep meaning. The meaning I got out of it was that he was weird and she didn't have a clue—so much for a 9-year-old's critique.

During most of the movie we hung out in the trees along the ditch bank. We had to keep an eye out for the man with the flashlight who patrolled the back fence. When he came by we jumped out of the trees and crawled into the tall weeds to wait for him to pass. Larry's mom had sent a bag of cookies with him. He divided them between us and we shared a soda pop I had taken from the fridge.

It got cold before the movie was over and since we had lost interest anyway, we headed back through the trees to our bikes before the movie let out. Way before my sister got home we were pushing our bikes back underneath the maple tree. We slipped over the fence and crawled into our sleeping bags.

5:00 a.m. came way too early the next morning. My dad came out to get me up so I wouldn't keep Mr. Jepson waiting. I was so tired and I really didn't want to get out of my warm bag but my dad tipped it upside down and dumped me on the ground. I crawled toward the house while my friends slept on into the morning.

Grabbing a bowl of hot cereal and a glass of milk I went out and sat on the front porch. Mr. Jepson arrived on time and I drug myself into the back of the truck and headed to work. Once I started running I woke up and forgot that I hadn't slept much.

That night I added up what I had earned. I had money from two lawn mowing jobs, a small tip, and money for two days at my **not** *so fun and run* job. The total came to $6.29. It didn't seem like much but now I had a newspaper route that would start in a few days. I could be making $14.00 a week— not good enough. I needed more lawns to mow; I still needed to find more jobs.

Thursday morning I woke up to find my sister gone to work and my mom and dad both gone to work early. Sitting on the counter was a bowl and a note. On the stove was a pot with some mush—it was still warm. I opened the fridge, pulled the milk out, filled my bowl and ate a quick breakfast.

With a full stomach, I decided it was time to get to work. I figured that if I knocked on every door in the neighborhood where I could see the yard needed attention, I was sure to line up a few more lawn mowing jobs. After a couple of hours I added up the jobs in my head. I had a total of 11 lawns to mow each week!

"Wow," I thought. *This is all coming together!* I went home to get the mower—some of my new jobs wanted their lawn cut right away.

The days were starting to get hotter as the summer progressed. I knew it was going to be a hot afternoon—especially for someone mowing lawns. The sun was already beating down on my head and my shirt was feeling sticky. I could feel the heat working its way through my boots as I walked. The sweat was filling in around my toes and I felt my pace slacken. This is not what I wanted to be doing. Closing my eyes, I focused my attention on the Big Red Bike. First, I saw it in the window; then I *felt* it underneath me as I rode through the neighborhood. That was all it took to get me going again. The intensity of the sun dissipated almost immediately and it didn't seem so hot any more.

Three lawns and three gallons of water later, I was out of gas—not only in the mower but I was tired and hungry. I was headed for home when my friends pulled around the corner on their bikes. There was something in their baskets but all I could see were blobs of color.

They stopped about 10 feet from me. Billy reached into his basket, pulled out a water balloon and chucked it at me drenching my shirt with cool water; Lonnie and Larry followed his lead. They plastered me before I could react. I circled them and managed to grab several balloons from their baskets to return fire. I hammered Larry on the back; Lonnie slammed one into the side of Billy's head; Larry retaliated hitting me in the chest; then we ran out of ammo. We were completely soaked and there was a brief pause in the action but then everyone spotted it at the same time.

On the lawn in front of us was a sprinkler diligently rotating back and forth. Pushing and shoving, we all ran for it. Billy tripped me and I grabbed Lonnie's leg. Larry reached it first, turning it on Billy who was right behind him. He fell to the ground laughing. I grabbed it from Larry and turned it on all three of them. "That's what you get for blasting me with water balloons!" I laughed.

Larry tackled me and Billy grabbed the sprinkler from me. I tried to roll away but Larry held tight and Billy forced the sprinkler straight into my face. "And that's what you get for working all day and deserting your friends!" he retorted.

We rolled in the water and threw grass at each other. Gosh it felt good to cool off with my friends. I was glad I hadn't scheduled any more lawns to mow today. Shaking the water from our hair and clothes we jumped up and headed to my house for Kool-Aid underneath the maple tree.

Chapter 10
The Big Battle

I opened the door and found that my sister had returned from work. "Will you make us some Kool-Aid?" I asked.

She was sitting in the kitchen with one of her friends. She nodded. A few minutes later she brought out orange Kool-Aid in a big plastic pitcher and some metal cups. I carried them to the tree where we had all found some shade. We talked about the go-cart and then about starting a baseball game on the front lawn, but nobody had a mitt.

"It's time we headed for the pond!" Billy blurted out all of a sudden. We all looked at each other and with wide grins on our faces we agreed. It was the perfect afternoon for a dip in the pond.

With dust trailing us, we rode four-across down the Bangerter trail to the swimming hole. We were laughing and ramming each other as we rode when Carlos and his older brother, Ricardo jumped out from the side of the trail. Fernando was with them. These guys were just about the meanest kids in town—and they had no love for us. We always fought with Carlos and Fernando over the basketball at school and when we played kickball, Billy always made sure the ball hit them in the head. With no way to go around them, we skidded to a stop. Billy got off his bike and stepped around in front of the rest of us.

"Get out of our way. NOW!" he bellowed.

I would have gotten out of the way if I had been Carlos, but Carlos and Billy had a long history that went back to the first grade. They had been in a number of fights and Carlos didn't know when to quit. Now that his older brother was with them, Carlos evidently thought he had the edge. His brother was four inches taller than any of us and weighed at least 30 pounds more than Billy. It looked like today was the day I had always known would come.

Lonnie was never a fighter. He looked nervously at the ground. I knew it was up to Larry, Billy, and me.

Ricardo advanced one step toward Billy. That was all it took. Billy kicked him right between the legs and he went down grabbing himself with both hands so fast that we didn't have time to think. But Billy didn't stop there. Before Ricardo hit the ground Billy was on top of him.

Carlos moved in to help his brother but Larry made a flying leap and caught him across the chest with his arm. Carlos fell over on his back. Fernando came at me but I was one move ahead of him. Without thinking, I swung. My fist caught him in the face and he went down holding his nose with both hands—blood gushing through his fingers. He took off as soon as he could get up and run.

Carlos was back on his feet in a hurry, grabbing at his brother's arm, trying to get him away from Billy. Larry shoved him away. Billy was a wild man flailing both fists until Ricardo rolled out from under him and staggered away still holding his crotch. As soon as Ricardo was on his feet, Carlos took off after him and they were gone.

Lonnie, now a bit braver, yelled at them. "Stay away from us or it will be it worse next time!"

Billy was sitting on the ground. He burst out laughing when he heard Lonnie telling them off. I was shaking so hard I could hardly stand up. It was the first real fight of my life. I had seen Billy fight and I had seen other fights at school, but I had never hit anyone like that before.

Billy got to his feet and admiring the blood on the front of my shirt, he put his arm around my neck. He reached over to Larry and did the same. With Lonnie standing in front of us, Billy declared, "That will be the last time we ever have to deal with them." He pulled us together and put his hand out in front of him. We laid our hands over his. "Three cheers for the toughest and meanest boys on the block," he hollered.

We joined in together, "Hooray! Hooray! Hooray!"

I didn't feel very tough. My hand hurt and I was still shaking like a milk shake but by the time we arrived at the pond my heart rate was back to normal.

We had a raft we had built the previous summer. It was hidden in the reeds along the edge of the pond. We found it and with the homemade wooden paddles we pushed it out to the middle of the pond. Leaving our shirts on the raft, we jumped, carefree, into the cool, refreshing water. Laughing and splashing, we basked in the joy of being 9-year-old boys.

After a few minutes, I climbed out of the water and sat on the edge of the raft. Larry joined me. A big dragonfly skimmed across the water. The beat of its wings resonated in a low hum across the pond. I laid back and looked up into the few clouds that were in the sky.

"That was quite a show back there wasn't it?" I said. "I was so scared I just hit him and didn't think about it. Do you think they'll try and get even?"

"I sure hope they don't," Larry laughed. "'Cause if I see them again I think I'll run the other direction. I don't think they would ever catch me."

As we dangled our feet in the water, the conversation eventually turned to the bike I was working so hard for. Larry was impressed with everything I had found to do to earn money. To be quite honest, I was impressed too. If it hadn't been for Mr. Paterson telling me to believe in my dreams, I would never have thought it was possible. Now, I was going to have that bike and I knew it. I pictured the Big Red Bike in my mind and described it to Larry with as much detail as I could. Just telling him about it gave me chills and I couldn't wait for him to see me riding it.

As the sun got lower in the sky we paddled the raft back to its hiding place. We got dressed and jumped on our bikes. Mine was working a lot better since I had fixed it up and I didn't get quite so far behind. In no time, we were all waving goodbye as I turned in the driveway and they rode on to their homes.

Chapter 11
Spudnuts and Shoe Shines

I was ready for bed even before it was time. It had been a big day and tomorrow was another **not** *so fun and run* day. My schedule was getting busier and busier. Besides running for Mr. Jepson, I had lined up two lawns to mow every day except Monday. On Monday I just had one. Then there was my paper route. It would begin this weekend. I thought about the Big Red Bike one last time before my head hit the pillow—then I was out.

In the morning I was sitting on the porch at 5:30. Mr. Jepson's truck pulled up and off we went. We worked the other side of town that morning and on the way home we went down Main Street. I saw a sign in the window of the Layton Bakery.

"Sell Spudnuts – Make $"

I knocked on the truck window and motioned for Mr. Jepson to pull over. I asked him to let me out and I told him I would walk home. He pulled out his clipboard and figured out my day's pay. Handing me the money, he rolled up his window, waved goodbye, and pulled away from the curb.

I ran across the street to the bakery. There was the sign that had caught my attention. I opened the door and the little bell that hung from the top of the door announced my arrival. Inside, was a glass counter with all kinds of cookies and doughnuts. Along the side wall were rows of freshly baked bread and rolls. The smell was enough to make any 9-year-old hungry—especially one who had been running for several hours. The wonderful smell reminded me of Saturday morning at home when my mother baked bread for the week. A fleeting thought went through my mind and for a split second I wondered if I could get away with the same trick I pulled at home. Could I cut one end of a loaf off and scoop out the middle—then put the end back? As soon as I thought about it, I remembered that I *didn't* get way with it at home. The last time I had tried, it had cost me a week of doing the dishes.

A very round, short man came from the back of the bakery. He was only about three inches taller than I was. He had a big bushy mustache and stubble on his face. He'd probably gotten up earlier than I had and he obviously hadn't taken the time to shave. Dusty flour powdered his white shirt and apron. Flour was on his face and in his eyebrows.

As he approached, I turned and pointed at the sign in the window. "How old do you have to be to get the job in the window?" I asked. "What are spudnuts, and how much money can I make selling them?" It all came out of my mouth at once.

He chuckled and reaching out his hand to me he inquired, "And your name is...?"

"Oh," I said, "I'm Jay and I live at the bottom of Hill Field Road." I could feel my face heat up and my cheeks turning red.

He reached inside the glass counter and handed me a cream-filled doughnut before he answered my questions. "There are several businesses in town that love to have fresh doughnuts in the morning, he explained." That's when I found out what spudnuts were.

"So spudnuts are just doughnuts?" I asked. "I thought they were something new."

He laughed out loud and his round belly jumped up and down like all the stories of Santa Clause I had heard. Little puffs of flour danced off his apron. He told me that the job involved going door to door to the businesses in the downtown area. If I had any left I could go to the houses in the neighborhood 'til I had sold them all. The pay was 10 cents for every bag I sold; there were 10 bags with a dozen in each bag.

"Okay," I told him. "I can be dropped off here on Mondays, Wednesdays, and Fridays."

"That's a problem then, Jay," he replied. "I need someone *every*day except the weekends."

"Well..." I said. Thinking it over, I finished the sentence, "then I will have to ride my bike here the other mornings."

He smiled, reached out his hand to shake on our deal and said, "You can start work right now!" He handed me a metal basket with a neck strap and filled it with white bags full of spudnuts. "The bank down the street is always good for one or two bags, Jay. I suggest you start there!"

I left the bakery and began another adventure. I had never sold anything before. I was nervous as I approached the bank doors. It was easy for me to talk to someone I knew but to walk up to a stranger was another thing. I opened the door. It was deathly quiet inside. The doors closed behind me. I walked up to the teller behind the counter. She had her back turned and hadn't seen me come in.

"Excuse me, Ma'am," I began. "Would you like to buy some spudnuts?"

"Well, hello there," she turned as she answered. "We haven't had anyone come in here for days. Sure we'll take a bag." She handed me the exact amount of money and let everyone know there were spudnuts available. "Did you just take over as spudnut salesman?"

"Yea, I guess I did," I replied. "Maybe I'll see you tomorrow."

That was easy, I thought as I left the bank and went outside. As I visited other businesses and a few homes, I found out that, for the most part, people were happy to talk with me. It was hard to get up the nerve to ask people if they wanted to buy some spudnuts but I figured once they knew me it would be a lot easier.

Two hours later, after walking into every store in town and then down a few side streets to the local neighbors, the spudnuts were finally sold. I walked back to the bakery feeling like I had really accomplished something. I had actually sold them all. I walked through the front door setting the metal basket down on a little table by the door. The bell tinkled as the door opened and the big round baker came to the front of the store. He was carrying a tray of big chocolate chip cookies. Setting them inside the glass, he glanced at the empty metal basket and smiled. I reached inside my pocket and pulled out a handful of dollar bills and a bunch of coins. I dropped it all in his hands.

When he had counted the money he handed me a $1.00 bill. "Good job. I'll see you in the morning, Jay."

I smiled putting the money in my pocket as I turned to leave.

"Wait, now," he said. "I have something for you." He went behind the counter and took two cookies and two spudnuts from underneath the glass counter and put them in a bag. Handing them to me he said, "Breakfast."

"Wow, thanks," I beamed and headed out the door to walk home.

I was walking down Main Street eating my cookies and spudnuts, wishing I had a tall glass of milk to go with them, when I glanced through the window of a barbershop. There were three men dressed in suits and two other guys in their farm coveralls. One of the men in a suit was wiping off his dusty shoes with a rag. His shoes were all scuffed up and he had a look of disgust on his face.

The next store down the street was the drug store. And right in the corner of the display window was a shoeshine kit. It was full of brushes and little cans of shoe polish. When you put the box lid down there was a place for someone to put their foot. Immediately, lights went off in my head. In my mind I heard, *You can earn lots of money shining shoes!*

I walked inside the store, wiping my sticky hands on my pants, and looked in the window at the shoe-shine kit. There was a price tag attached with a string that hung from the side of the box. I reached down and turned it over. To my surprise it was on sale! The regular price had been crossed out and a sale price was written underneath it. It was on sale for $3.59.

I reached inside my pocket and pulled out the day's earnings. I had a dollar from spudnut sales and $1.55 from running flyers. There were two quarters from the day before—a total of $3.05.

The lady from the front counter could see me counting my money. She walked up to me and asked, "Can I help you, lad?"

I looked up at her, "I want to buy this kit here but I only have $3.05."

She leaned over my shoulder and picked up the tag. She looked back at me and said, "This has been here since Christmas and my husband wants it sold. So, for you, this shoeshine kit is on sale for $3.05!" She closed the box and took it to the cash register. I laid my money on the counter while she removed the price tag and then slid the box toward me. With a smile, she wished me good luck.

I took the box outside and opened it up. It had six different colors of polish, a brush to put the polish on, a big black brush to shine the shoes, and six polishing rags—one for each color of polish. There were instructions with pictures of each step. I looked down at my own boots. They were bare to the leather. Sitting down beneath a tree, I took off my boots and followed the directions from the kit. In about 10 minutes they looked good enough to wear to church.

Feeling like I knew what to do, I packed everything up and closed the box. I went back up the street past the drug store to the barbershop. There were three different men inside now. I looked in at their shoes. They all needed a shine so I walked inside—the bell above the door tinkled as I entered.

The barber looked over at me and seeing the shoeshine box he asked, "You shine shoes boy?"

I gave him my most confident smile and said, "I can shine anybody's shoes for only 25 cents."

He looked around at his customers and asked if anyone wanted their shoes shined while they waited.

All three men answered in the affirmative. "My shoes haven't been shined in weeks," said the first man. I sat down in front of him, opened up my box and got to work.

It wasn't long before I finished, collected my fee and moved on to the next man ...and the next. The last man was getting his hair cut when I started to shine his shoes. When I was finished, he pulled out a big shiny 50-cent piece and flipped it into the air. "Thanks boy, they look very nice," he said.

As I was about to leave, the barber looked my way and said, "We have businessmen here every day between 11:00 and 1:00. Can you be here to do this everyday?"

"I'll do my best sir." I replied. "I have other jobs but I'll do my best to be here."

I thought about the shoeshine kit as I went out the door. I had spent $3.05 and I had made $1.00 the first day—not a bad return for a one day investment.

I knew where I was headed before I even got started. The way home took me right past the bicycle shop. There in the front window was the reason I was giving up my entire summer. The Big Red Bike stood like a shining giant in the window. I stood there for the longest time, just looking at it. For some reason, no matter where the sun was in the sky, light danced off the chrome fenders and handlebars sending flickers in every direction.

I can't wait 'til it's mine and I can ride it home. I thought.

Mr. Paterson saw me from the sidewalk and came to the window motioning for me to come in. He always had that red rag in his hands. Today he wore a blue jacket over his white shirt and a blue striped tie. The tie was loose around his neck.

The cool air gushed past me as I pushed hard on the door. It felt good. I walked back to meet Mr. Paterson and I sat down on a stool at the counter placing the shoe-shine kit at my feet. He reached over and opened an old refrigerator and handed me a *Nehi* orange drink. I opened the bottle using the opener that was attached to the end of the counter. Then I put my elbows up on the counter, let out a big sigh, and took one giant swig of the cold drink.

Mr. Paterson sat down next to me and leaned forward. "When are you going to come for that new bike, Jay? It's waiting for you. In fact, every time I think I have it sold, something happens and they choose another bike."

Whew, I thought. "That's because that bike is mine, sir, and I am doing everything I can to get the money."

He asked me what I was doing, so I told him everything that was happening.

"I have five different jobs, Mr. Paterson," I said. "I mow 11 lawns each week. I pass out door hangers three mornings each week for a penny a door. I just got a paper route. And this morning I got a job selling spudnuts—and another job shining shoes." I motioned in the direction of the shoeshine kit I had placed on the floor. When I finished telling him everything, his mouth was hanging open, his eyes were large, and he let out a gasp of surprise.

"You really want that bike don't you?" he said.

"More than anything, Mr. Paterson!" I took another big swallow from my *Nehi* orange and spilled some on his counter. He reached over with his red rag and wiped it up.

He thought for a minute and then he asked, "Do you want to take it for a ride?"

I nearly fell off the stool. "Can I? Really?"

He stood up and ruffled my hair. He walked to the front of the store and pulling the bike down from the window, he carefully took off the big price tag, kicked back the kickstand and brought it to the front door. He handed the bike over to me and opened the door for me to take it out.

I walked the Big Red Bike through the door into the parking lot. I put my leg up over the top bar and with a little push I started down the sidewalk heading for a bigger parking lot down the street. Around and around I went shifting from first gear to second gear and back again. (I couldn't get enough speed to make it to the third gear in the parking lot.) The wind was blowing through my hair and the breeze filled my soul with joy each time I went around the lot. It was like riding on a cloud after riding *The Monster*. The springs underneath the seat bounced as I stood up and sat down.

After 15 minutes of heaven, I rode back to where Mr. Paterson was leaning against the building. I think he enjoyed watching me as much as I enjoyed the chance to ride the bike. As I slid off the seat and handed the bike back to Mr. Paterson I hesitated for a moment. I wanted to hold on as long as I could. He pushed the bike back into the store and lifted it onto the window stand, hanging the price tag once again on the handlebars.

I felt like something had been taken away from me.

"You just let me know when you're ready, Jay, and I'll have it ready for you!" he said as he pulled the red rag from his back pocket and began to polish up the bike.

I grabbed the shoe-shine kit and was just about out the door when he turned around and asked me, "How much money have you earned so far?"

I thought about if for a second and said, "I have about $8.00."

"Keep working and count it all up. Next time you are out this way come see me again."

I waved goodbye and hurried out the door. I still had two lawns to mow and I had told Phil Fox I would be there to help him do the paper route. Today was the day he was going to show me everything before he left town. My day was not over yet.

Chapter 12
SOLD!

I arrived home with a couple of hours to spare before I had to meet Phil. I didn't even go in the house. I figured I had just enough time to mow both lawns before the newspapers arrived. I went to the garage and topped off the gas tank in the lawn mower—then hurried down the street. The first lawn was way overgrown and I thought I'd never get through it, but the second one went quickly. I was glad for that because as I was finishing up I saw the newspaper delivery truck head down the street to drop off the newspapers in Phil's driveway.

Phil had already started rolling the papers when I got there. His parents were busy packing a big truck with boxes. Phil showed me how to stack the papers in a bag and how to wrap the bag around the handle bars so it wouldn't get caught in the tires. He had drawn a map of the whole neighborhood for me so I'd know which houses to deliver to. Every house that was supposed to get a paper had a check in front of it. The ones that took the Sunday paper had two checks. The ones that didn't take the paper had an "X" through them.

We refilled the bag with papers three times before we had delivered them all. After we finished, we went back to his house. Phil went inside and came back with a black book like a school binder. He sat down on the steps and showed me the record book. There was a page for each person who took the paper. He showed me how to keep track of everything—when to collect for the papers and how to make payments to the newspaper company. Finally we stood up. I was now the official newspaper delivery boy for the neighborhood. Route # 744.

When I got home that night it was 7:30. I hadn't been home since 5:30 that morning except to grab the lawn mower. Both my sister and my dad were sitting on the steps in front of the house. My dad had a worried look on his face and when my sister saw me she started to yell.

"Where have you been, Jay? I have been looking for you *all* day!"

It had been a couple of days since I had really had a chance to talk with anyone at home. I started by telling them about my day—about the spudnut selling and the money I had earned shining shoes. My sister calmed down and my dad just looked at me.   Then I told them how many lawn mowing jobs I had lined up, and finally I told them about the newspaper route. That got my dad's attention. He had a lot of questions.

"Let me see if I understand this right," he said. "You are the new paperboy in the neighborhood and you start delivering papers tomorrow evening?"

"Yup," I said pushing my chest out as I took in a deep breath.

"Well, son, this is a big responsibility. I hope you understand that it means you will have to be here everyday to get the papers prepared."

"I know, dad." I was real serious. "I really want the bike. Mr. Paterson even let me ride it today."

I told my dad that I had walked past the bike shop on my way home and how Mr. Paterson had let me ride it around the parking lot. My dad just kept looking at me. I wasn't sure what he was thinking.

He changed the subject back to the paper route. "Does this include delivering the Sunday morning paper?" he asked, "...because there is no way you can deliver all those big papers that early in the morning on your bike before church. I don't want to be the one doing the job when you can't get it done on your own."

I hadn't really thought about Sunday—or the fact that the Sunday papers had to be delivered early in the morning. I didn't have an answer for my dad. "I don't know how I'll take care of Sunday," I said.

He stood up. "Well, then we'll have to work it out as we go."

We went in the house and I brought out my little notebook for dad to see. I flipped it to the page where I had been keeping track of all my different jobs.

"Look at this dad," I said, holding my notebook out for him to read. "I have 11 lawns to mow every week—that's $11.00 a week and sometimes more if I pull weeds. Three days a week I run for Mr. Jepson—that's about $4.50 a week. Now I'm selling spudnuts every day—that's another $5.00 a week. Then there's shoe shining and my paper route. I can do it, dad!" I told him optimistically. "I didn't think I could do it, but now I *know* I can make enough money to buy the bike!"

"Well then, Jay," my father said with a smile, "I guess you'd better get in the kitchen and get some dinner. It looks like you have a few big weeks ahead of you."

After dinner I showed my mom and dad the shoeshine kit. I explained how much I had paid for it and how much I had earned in just one day.

I could tell they were proud of me and maybe just a bit concerned. I'm sure they were wondering whether I could keep up with everything. Honestly? I was wondering the same thing.

Sunday was *really* hard. The papers arrived at 4:00 a.m. It took six trips on my bike to finish the route and get home for church—but I did it! It was hard staying awake in church. I tried to keep at least one eye open, but mostly I had both eyes closed. I remember walking out to the car with my parents—then I fell asleep on the three block drive home.

The rest of the week was just as hard. It was one of the hardest weeks of my young life. Monday I was up early running for Mr. Jepson. I sold spudnuts and shined four pair of shoes at the barbershop. I cut one lawn. Then I got the papers delivered before I crashed in bed right after dinner. Tuesday I slept in (if you call 7:30 sleeping in). After breakfast, I rode my bike into town to sell spudnuts and shine shoes—then home to mow lawns and deliver papers. Wednesday I was up early again, running, then selling spudnuts, shoe shining, mowing lawns, and delivering papers. (You get the idea.) I didn't see my friends all week.

On Thursday night I sat down to add up everything I had earned. I was planning to visit Mr. Paterson on my way home from town. I pulled out money from my pockets and from my drawer. I unfolded all the paper bills and laid out all the change on my bed. When I finished counting I just shook my head. I had $35.00!! I couldn't wait to show Mr. Paterson.

On my way home after shining shoes Friday afternoon, I stopped at the bike shop.

I was so excited to have Mr. Paterson see how hard I'd been working on earning the money for the bike that I ran the last block. There in the front window was the Big Red Bike. But there was something else. My heart slammed into my chest. A big yellow tag hung from the handlebars of the bike. In bold, capital letters it said, SOLD!

I didn't know whether to scream or to cry. *How could this happen?* I asked myself, *...and after all my hard work?*

I sat down on the sidewalk in front of the bike shop and let the tears fall. I felt as if everything in the world had been taken from me. I was hurt; I was angry; and I was sad all at the same time.

The emptiness in my stomach was terrible and I had to put my hands underneath my legs to keep them from trembling.

I must have been there for quite a while because when I looked down, my shirt was wet with tears. Disappointed beyond anything I had ever experienced, I stood up to leave. I could see Mr. Paterson through the window with a customer. He saw me at the same moment and waved his hand for me to come in as he said goodbye to his customer.

I didn't want to talk to him. I didn't want anyone to see me cry and I knew that talking would only bring more tears.

Again, he waved for me to come in but I couldn't move. I just stood there. When the customer left the store Mr. Paterson walked out to where I stood. Putting his arm around my shoulder he gently pulled me in and guided me to a stool at the back counter. He opened the refrigerator and brought me a grape *Nehi* soda. I opened it using the opener on the side of the counter and set it down in front of me. My insides were churning so much that I wasn't sure I could drink anything.

Wiping my face with my sleeve and trying to hold back the tears, I looked up at Mr. Paterson through red eyes, "You sold my bike." My voice quivered even though I tried to keep it strong.

"Yes I did, Jay ...right after you left last week. I've been waiting for the fellow to come back and pick it up," he explained.

There was a long silence and I finally got the courage to ask, "Who bought it? Is it someone I know?" I couldn't bear the thought of having someone in the neighborhood riding *my* bike.

"I think you know him," he said.

My heart sank clear to my feet and my eyes fell to the floor. I didn't dare ask who it was. I wanted to know—but at the same time I didn't want to know.

Mr. Paterson opened the fridge again and took out another drink for himself. As he popped the lid on the opener, the fizz broke a long silence. He opened a drawer from behind the counter and lifted out a piece of paper. "What have you been doing this past week, Jay? I was sure I would have seen you sooner than this."

I told him how busy I had been. I explained that the reason I hadn't been back to see him was because I was working so hard to earn the money for the bike.

"How much have you saved up so far?" he asked.

I reached into my pocket and pulled out a wad of bills and change. Only a few minutes earlier I had been so excited to see his face when he discovered how much I had earned. Now it didn't really matter. We counted the money silently together. The total came to $38.75.

"Wow, Jay," Mr. Paterson said. "You really have been working hard. I never expected to see this much ...and you know what?" He asked.

"What?" I answered flatly.

He paused and looked deeply into my eyes making sure that he had my full attention.

In a louder voice he said, "It's just enough money for a down payment on a bike." He grabbed a pen from his shirt pocket and wrote down $38.75 on the paper he had pulled from the drawer. He slid it in my direction.

I looked down at the paper. The first thing I saw were the capital letters at the top of the page: **PURCHASE CONTRACT**.

"So, he feels bad about selling the bike and he's going to let me buy another one," I thought. *"But I don't want another bike. I want the Big Red Bike in the window."* I continued to read:

This contract is between Paterson Schwinn Bicycle Shop and <u>Mr. Jay Tims </u>for the sum of $129.95 plus tax for a total of $132.81. *(I remembered that $129.95 was the price of the Big Red Bike and my heart started to beat faster and faster. I kept reading.)* **... for the purchase of a red Schwinn, Mark II Jaguar bicycle: serial number #4485492.** *(I could hardly make myself read each word as I hurried to get to the end.)*

Mr. Tims agrees to pay a down payment of <u>$38.75</u> with a balance due of <u>$ </u>. Payments are due each

**Friday, determined by Mr. Tims weekly earnings until
the balance is paid in full.**

**The above named bike will be owned by Paterson
Schwinn Bicycle shop until such time as the balance is
paid in full.**

There was a place for both our signatures at
the bottom of the contract.

My mouth fell open. "You mean the bike was
sold to me?" I asked, incredulous. As I asked the
question I leaned over to shift my weight on the
stool but the fireworks going off in my head and
heart made me dizzy with excitement. I literally
fell on the floor.

Mr. Paterson nodded with a grin so big I
thought his cheeks would burst. ...I thought *my*
cheeks would burst!!

I jumped to my feet—and kept jumping ...and
jumping. I let out yelps of joy clenching my fists
above my head. I couldn't contain myself. "Yes!" I
yelled over and over again. Every limb in my body
was twitching with delight.

Mr. Paterson was laughing as loudly as I was yelling and I noticed that his eyes started to glisten as he danced with me in the middle of the bicycle shop floor.

I ran to the Big Red Bike. I was shaking with excitement as I picked up the yellow tag hanging from the handlebars. In small print underneath the letters spelling out the word "SOLD" was my name. Sold to: *Jay Tims,* it said. It had been mine all along and I had completely missed it.

Mr. Paterson reached around me and helped me lift the bike to the floor. We removed the tags and wheeled it to the back room where he put it up on the workbench and began to teach me everything I needed to know about taking care of the Big Red Bike—MY Big Red Bike.

We oiled the chain and put some black graphite powder inside the shifter on the handle. He showed me how to put new batteries in the headlight and tail light. We tightened each screw and bolt as he explained to me how everything was meant to function. He made sure everything was perfect. Then, lifting the bike back to the floor, I sat on the seat as he adjusted it for my height. I watched carefully so I would understand everything.

He wheeled the bike to the counter where he stopped. Reaching for the contract he calculated the amount due, wrote it in the blank, and signed his name. Then he handed the pen to me. My hand was shaking. I had never signed a contract before. Carefully, I wrote in my best cursive writing, *Jay Tims*. I pushed the contract back to Mr. Paterson.

At that moment, I left the world of a child and entered the world of a grown-up where being responsible was one of the most important things I could do. I turned around and without thinking, I gave Mr. Paterson a big hug around the waist. He patted me gently on the shoulder.

Now the tears were streaming down my cheeks. I couldn't stop them and I didn't care. I looked up into his face—a face so kind that I will never forget it as long as I live.

We pushed the bike out the front door. Then, swinging my leg up over the bar I pushed off with the other foot and slid comfortably into the seat. I pushed hard on the pedals and the bike surged forward. It was so nice to push down hard and not worry about the chain coming off. As I built up speed, I shifted into second gear. I was absolutely in heaven.

I turned around and saw Mr. Paterson still standing in front of the bike shop. He waved me on my way. I waved back with my free hand as I held the handlebars with the other. I turned and shifted into third gear. Riding the Big Red Bike was exactly as it had been in my dreams—effortless. Each time I pushed down on the pedals the bike glided forward. I was flying!!

All I wanted to do—for the rest of my life—was to ride my new bike. I wanted to show it to my friends and I wanted them to see *me* riding it. But as I rode into the driveway, I realized how late it was. I still had two lawns to mow and it would not be long before the papers would be sitting in my driveway. Responsibility had its price.

I put my new bike carefully inside the garage and pulled the lawn mower out. I filled the gas tank and glanced over my shoulder at my new bike one last time as I pushed the mower down the street. I wondered how I would explain the bike to my parents. They worked so hard for everything they had. *Would they be happy for me?* I wondered, *...or would they be disappointed that I hadn't earned the money first, before I got the bike?* It was hard to tell.

I finished both lawns and rounded the corner with the mower. The papers were already sitting in the driveway. Putting the lawn mower away, I stared at the Big Red Bike on the other side of the garage. It was so incredible! I walked over and turned on the headlight. A bright beam shone on the wall of the garage. I turned on the tail light and another beam shot out in the other direction hitting the opposite wall. I couldn't wait to ride it delivering papers. Bringing it to the front yard, I put down the kickstand and turned off the head and tail lights. I returned to the garage to get the rubber bands and the delivery bag and just then three bikes came screeching to a halt in front of my house.

Billy, Larry, and Lonnie all saw the bike at the same moment. They dropped their bikes on the lawn and walked up to "Big Red." Nobody said a word as they ran their fingers up and down the frame and across the 3-speed control box.

Finally, Billy shook his head and sat down cross-legged in front of the bike. "So, you really did it didn't you? How did you get your dad to buy the bike for you?"

I couldn't wait to tell them everything. I grabbed a pile of papers, sat down by Billy in front of the bike and began to roll up papers and put rubber bands on them while I talked. "My dad *didn't* buy it." I said. "My dad doesn't even know I've got it yet. Mr. Paterson sold it to me ...on a contract!"

Billy reached over to grab a paper and a few rubber bands to help. Larry and Lonnie grabbed a few too. We sat there rolling papers together while I told them the whole story.

And *then* the rest of my dream came true. They all begged me to let them ride my new red bike.

Chapter 13
Mr. Paterson

That night when I got home after finishing my paper route I pulled in the driveway to find my dad working in the garage. He looked up at me sitting on that beautiful red bike and his mouth dropped to his chest.

He put down his tools and asked, "How did you get that bike, Jay?" There was concern in his voice.

I pushed the bike into the garage and put the kickstand down. There were several dozen bats that had begun to fly around in my stomach. I took a deep breath as I pushed the hair from my eyes and began to explain.

"You know how I've been saving money to buy this bike, dad," I began. "Mr. Paterson and I have been talking about it. When I went into the bike shop this afternoon he had a contract all written up with my name on it and everything. He took the money I've made—as a down payment—and he let me take the bike! So, it's mine, dad—fair and square—as soon as I finish paying for it! I already paid him $38.75."

My dad just looked at me. It was the same look he had on his face when I told him about the paper route and all the other jobs I had found to earn money for the bike. "You've already paid him $38.75?" he asked shaking his head.

"Yes," I told him, nodding.

"That's incredible ...it's absolutely incredible," he said almost to himself, still shaking his head.

"I had no idea you would continue to work this hard for that bike."

My dad paused again. I knew he was thinking real hard about something. "Well, son," he said finally as a broad smile crept over his face. "I've never seen a kid so determined in all my life." He leaned down and looked into my eyes as he laid his arm around my shoulder. "You *deserve* to have that bike—that's all there is to it! But just remember that you have made a *big* commitment to Mr. Paterson and you still have a long way to go before it's paid for. Just because you're riding it around doesn't mean it's yours until it's paid for—understand?"

"Yes, dad," I said. I was jumping for joy inside. My dad was going to let me keep it!

"Jay," he said. "There is something I want you to understand. Your name is on that contract, and your name is your honor. Don't ever let me find out that you've slacked off in making your payments to Mr. Paterson. That would be the biggest disappointment of my life. Hear me?"

"Yes, dad," I said. I reached out with both arms and held him tightly. I knew how important it was to finish what I had started. Dad had taught me that too.

I had a different dream that night: *I was riding down the street on Big Red—riding to all my different jobs—only no matter where I went, my dad was on someone's porch or in some shop watching me.*

From that day forward my friends—even Billy—had a little more respect for me. I had accomplished something that no kid they knew had ever accomplished. In some ways, that made me a grown-up in their eyes. They asked my opinion about things that never would have come up in our conversations before. In other subtle ways they treated me differently. I had taken a big step forward in my life. They knew it and I knew it.

Having Big Red was everything I had dreamed it would be. Just riding it made me feel like a million dollars—and that was a continual reminder to me that I still owed Mr. Paterson quite a bit of money. I kept up my rigorous schedule for most of the summer—until I had made the final payment. That meant that I saw my friends less and less.

Each week on Friday I stopped at the bike shop to drop off my payment. Mr. Paterson kept a running total in his desk drawer. If there were no customers in the store he always took time to sit down with me and ask me about my week: What were my friends and I up to? Had I had a chance to ride the go-cart? Was I taking good care of my bike?—he always asked me that question. Often he brought out a soda from the little refrigerator behind the counter and we had a drink together. He shared his week with me too, and I always knew what was new in the world of bicycles. He became one of the few adults that I could call a real friend.

Most of the time I was on foot when I came to make my payments but one week I rode up and parked my bike on the sidewalk just outside the front door. Mr. Paterson saw me ride up and came out to meet me. He took one look at my bike and chewed me out—not in a mean way but he let me know that I wasn't taking very good care of my bike.

"Jay, do you remember what that bike looked like when you saw it for the first time in the store window?" he asked.

"Yes, it was the most beautiful thing I had ever seen in my life!" I told him.

"Well, this bike doesn't look anything like the bike I sold you a few weeks ago. It looks like it belongs to someone who doesn't care very much about it. Is that the way you feel?"

"No! I love this bike more than anything, Mr. Paterson," I assured him. But I knew what he was talking about. I had ridden my bike in the rain and there was mud everywhere. The grease from the chain was mixed with mud and the bike had collected dust since the rain. I hadn't cleaned it since I brought it home from the bike shop. I really didn't have much time with all the jobs I was doing, but Mr. Paterson didn't let me get away with that excuse.

He went in the back room of the shop and brought me a red grease rag just like the one he always carried in his back pocket. "Here," he said as he handed the rag to me. "This is yours. I want you to use it to keep this bike looking just like it did when you took it home for the first time. If you take care of your belongings, Jay, they will take care of you for a long time. And you'll feel good about yourself too."

Then, together, Mr. Paterson and I cleaned and polished my bike from fender to fender. We greased the chain and oiled all the moving parts. When we were finished, it looked great. Mr. Paterson was a smart man and he was right, I felt proud. I never let him see my bike that dirty again—ever.

Several weeks later when I went in to make my weekly payment, I noticed a stack of big flat boxes in the back room. Mr. Paterson was with a customer but he motioned for me to sit down and wait for him.

"How would you like to help me for a while? he asked when the customer had gone. "Do you have some time?"

"Sure, I have time," I said. I liked spending time with Mr. Paterson. *I'll have to hurry to mow a couple of lawns before the papers arrive,* I thought to myself, but the time I spent with Mr. Paterson was always worth it.

"Come and help me put this new bike together. He nudged me gently, motioning for me to come in the back where the boxes were. "Let's see if you've learned anything while you've been hanging around here!"

He handed me a pair of pliers and a small knife and I started to pull out staples and cut through straps to open the box.

"This is a brand new one from Schwinn. I want to get in the front window right away."

As we tore down the boxes and the bike revealed itself, I could see that it was a lot like my bike. It had the same chrome fenders and a lot of the same features but it was coal black.

"Nice," I said to Mr. Paterson, but in my mind there was no way it compared to *Big Red*.

As we opened each box, we laid the parts out across the floor so we could see which parts went with which part of the bike. He set the frame upside down on the workbench so that it sat on its handlebars, then he slid the tool cart over to the side of us and sat down on a stool.

"Okay, Jay. Where would you start?"

I reached over and picked up the front wheel, fastening it into the fork on the front frame with the bolts that were with it. Then I picked up the back tire and pulled the chain out of the box it was still in. Slipping the wheel into the frame, I tightened the bolts down just enough to hold it in place so that I could position the chain. I looked up for his approval.

Mr. Paterson nodded and continued to watch as I worked. I began to wonder if this was a test. I guessed that he would tell me if I did anything wrong. After a few minutes I got to a point where I didn't know what to do. I'd never built a bike from scratch before and I wasn't quite sure what came next. I looked up for suggestions.

"You're doing great, Jay," Mr. Paterson said. "Need some help?"

"Yea," I said. "I thought we were going to do this together."

Mr. Paterson let out a laugh. "I was just waiting for you to ask."

"Oh," I replied. "I thought it was a test."

Mr. Paterson laughed again. He leaned back on his stool. "Watching you figure out how to put a bike together reminds me that almost every day I do something I've never done before. Do you believe that, Jay?"

"I guess I never thought about it." I said. "I thought grown-ups knew pretty much everything."

"Well, they don't, Jay. There are lots of things grown-ups don't know. The trick is to know when you don't know something—and the other part of it is—not to be afraid to ask."

"I think I know what you mean, Mr. Paterson," I said, reflectively.

We finished putting the bike together and Mr. Paterson placed it in the front window. It looked nice but it didn't hold a candle to my bike. To this day the only bike I can see in the bike shop window is *Big Red*.

Chapter 14
The Race

The afternoon was hot and muggy as the sun poked out from behind a mass of dark clouds. The air was still thick after the summer thundershower and an occasional few drops of rain still fell into puddles on the sidewalk. I was sitting on the front porch rolling my papers when Billy came speeding around the corner into the yard. He slammed on his brakes and slid sideways to a stop, just inches away.

"Aren't you afraid you'll get that new bike of yours all wet and dirty, Jay?" The smile on his face took on that sinister look I hated. With one foot, he reached out and gave *Big Red* a shove. The weight of the papers in the bag hanging from the handlebars made it an easy target and it began to fall.

I reached out to catch the bike but connected with Billy's other foot as he caught me off balance sending me into the flower bed off the edge of the porch. My blood started to boil as I reached out my hand to get up. But each time I got to my knees Billy pushed me back into the mud. He always made sure he had the upper hand and today was no different.

Billy had gotten increasingly aggressive in the weeks since I had brought home my new bike. He was used to making fun of *The Monster* and now that I had gotten *Big Red,* he was jealous. He couldn't stand it that I had a better bike than he did and he took every opportunity to put me down. No longer able to make fun of my old bike, he had turned on me.

"You think you're too good for us, now don't you?" Billy sneered. "But I've figured it out and I don't believe you bought that bike. Mr. Paterson just felt sorry for you. He *gave* that bike to you—didn't he? He knows your folks can't buy you a new bike. They don't make enough money to get you a real pair of pants."

I turned and pulled myself around to face him. I wanted to jump down his throat and make him shut up. I wanted to wipe the sneer from his face with one good punch and see what he looked like with two missing front teeth. But as I sat there in the mud, I remembered how hard he had hit Ricardo on the way to the pond—and I remembered that it wasn't just *one* punch. "What do you want from me Billy? Did your mom put starch in your underwear or are you just jealous?"

"Shut up Jay. You're asking for it. You don't want to find out how mad I can get." He slid off his bike and leaned over me with one fist clenched.

I just sat there and stared into his eyes. I wasn't going to show him that I was afraid, but I wasn't going to throw the first punch either—not when I was already on the ground. If he hit me then I would fight back, even if he turned me into hamburger. I could feel every muscle in my body tighten.

Billy towered over me, his straight dark hair falling into his eyes. He made a quick movement in my direction and I closed my eyes—not flinching but expecting the worst. When I didn't feel my nose break, I opened my eyes to see his hand reaching down to help me up.

I never understood Billy. He could be angry one minute and be your friend the next. He could turn it on and off like a light switch. Luckily for me, the light switch had been turned off, but I knew it wouldn't stay off forever. Ignoring his hand, I pushed myself up onto my knees and got up. "I have work to do, Billy," I said as I picked up my bike so the papers wouldn't get wet on the ground where they had fallen.

"You think that bike of yours is so great but I'll bet I can beat you in a race," he declared all of a sudden.

So this was what it was all about! Billy wanted to *prove* he was better than me. "A race?" I asked. "What for?"

"I'll bet you a month's allowance that I can beat you—Larry and Lonnie too—unless you're too afraid to lose your money—too afraid that bike of yours isn't good enough."

I stepped over to the porch and sat down, being careful to keep my distance and stay at least an arm's length away from Billy. I looked up and saw a flicker of sadness cross his face. It surprised me. *Why was he doing this?* I wondered. "Okay, I'll race you. But I'm not going to bet any money on it. I'll race you—but not for money."

Billy laughed, throwing his head back. "You *are* a chicken aren't you? You have the new bike—the one that's supposed to be so great—but you won't bet on it."

This was Billy's favorite thing to do. He would taunt people until they were so mad they'd do whatever he wanted them to. But I had seen it too often and I wasn't going to take the bait. "Sorry Billy," I said. "*Big Red* will beat you in a heartbeat but I'm not betting my money on it. You'd just love to see me get in trouble for missing a payment to Mr. Paterson, wouldn't you?"

Billy walked over and sat down next to me, making me slide over to the edge of the porch. "Relax," he said as I eyed him with caution. "All right then, since you're afraid to bet your money, I'll bet you my baseball glove against yours that I can win any race with you on that bike."

Thinking about the old worn-out glove sitting on the end of my bed, I answered, "All right, fine with me. But if you loose, I get your new glove, right?"

Billy put his arm around my shoulder and pulled me in close. He grinned and said, almost in a whisper, "If you win—and you won't—then it's yours. But you and I both know you will never win. Never."

I got up. "I'll call the guys right now," I said. "We can meet after my paper route tonight and plan the race."

Back then we had what was called a "party line"—a phone line that we shared with several other families. It was difficult to get an open line and I hardly ever called anyone. Today, I picked up the phone and couldn't believe the line was free. The operator asked what number I wanted. "Give me 4403," I answered, and within a few seconds Larry's mom was on the phone.

"Can I speak with Larry?" I asked.

After I had explained everything, Larry said he could meet us in a couple of hours. He agreed to call Lonnie so I could get started on my papers. I hung up the phone.

"We're meeting here in two hours," I told Billy. "I've got to get my paper route finished, so I have to hurry."

He laughed as he took off down the road. "You might want to get that glove all polished up for me. It's as good as mine."

Two hours later, I rode *Big Red* into the yard. The sky was darkening again and by the smell in the air, I could tell we were in for another rainstorm.

There were three bikes lying on the grass under the maple tree.

"The race is this Saturday at 10:00 in the morning," announced Billy. "We'll *hunt and run* after the race."

"Where are we going to race?" I asked. I sat down on the grass which was still damp from the afternoon rain.

Larry pulled a hand-drawn map from his shirt pocket and laid it out in front of me. A dark line marked the route through the streets he had drawn. We would head out to Hill Field Road; then up the hill to the farm road; down the farm road about a mile; up toward the mountains 'til we met the road coming back to the neighborhood. It would be a long race—about four miles—but they had chosen a good route. The last leg of the race included three steep hills. *Perfect*, I thought to myself.

Because I had never really let my friends ride *Big Red* that much, they didn't realize what an advantage I had—especially on hills. With three speeds, I could shift into first gear and climb hills with much less effort. When it came to going downhill, they could only go as fast as their pedals would take them. I could shift into third gear and the race would be mine. None of them had any idea.

We parted company as the rain started to pound the ground with large droplets. I pushed my bike into the garage and watched as everyone rode hard to get home before they got completely soaked. Thinking about it, I realized Billy couldn't have set himself up in a worse way. I wondered what the consequences might be when he realized it.

Friday night when I finished my paper route, I pulled out the oil can and spent time going over every part of my bike—just like Mr. Paterson had taught me. I oiled all the moving parts and checked everything before I went in for the night. It was hard to sleep. I was excited and I was nervous at the same time.

I was up early Saturday morning. I had to get one lawn mowed before the race. Within minutes of when I had put the lawn mower away, everyone arrived. "Let's get this race going," I said as I put a belt around my waist with an old army canteen full of water.

We pushed our bikes to the middle of the road. Billy, always making sure he had the advantage, pushed off as he yelled, "GO!" He was two bike lengths ahead of us before we got started.

We pulled out of the neighborhood onto Hill Field Road. The incline up the hill was gradual but it got steeper as it went. About halfway up the hill, Billy stood up on the pedals pumping hard to stay well ahead of me. Even though he was stronger than I was, he was already working hard. I decided to let him set the pace and to stay several bike lengths behind him. Larry and Lonnie were already way behind, but this wasn't their race. They had nothing to prove. They were just *along for the ride*.

The hill got steeper and I shifted into first gear. I had to hold back to keep from gaining on Billy who was working harder than ever. I was enjoying myself as the first leg of the race came to an end. We turned onto the old farm road. Looking back over my shoulder, I could see Larry and Lonnie talking and laughing as they slowly worked their way up the hill.

Billy was breathing hard and I noticed that he kept wiping sweat from his face. I was hot too, but I wasn't sweating like Billy. My new bike and I were a great team. I also realized that lugging heavy papers around to do my paper route had made my legs strong.

About three quarters of the way through the race I decided it was time to see what *Big Red* and I could do. I knew Billy was tired and I knew the last part of the race was mine. I shifted into second gear as I went around the corner. Then, I stood up and pedaled hard for the first time in the race. *Big Red* surged forward and I went past Billy like he was standing still. I would love to have looked back to see the expression on his face but I kept my focus. I shifted into third gear and tore off down the road. Then I sat down on the seat and let the bike take me.

The road flew past and the wind plastered my hair against my forehead. My sweaty shirt felt cool as the wind blew through my clothes. I could see the intersection ahead that took us back to the neighborhood. I slowed down to make the turn and reached back to grab my canteen for a drink. As I put it back onto my belt, I glanced over my shoulder. I was surprised to see how far I had pulled ahead. Billy was about 100 yards behind me and working harder than I had ever seen him work. His face was bright red. Larry and Lonnie were so far back I could barely see them.

As I went around the corner, I took in a deep breath. The air smelled of cows, pasture, and summer hay. Kicking back, I shifted into second gear—then into third as I gained speed going down the first of the three hills on the final leg of the race. I wanted to get as much speed as possible to carry me up the next big hill.

My legs burned, even in first gear, as I ground my way up the hill. I wondered what it would have been like on my old bike. I also wondered what it was like for Billy and the others with only one speed. I stood up and pumped hard to make it to top of the hill. As I pushed my way over the crest, I turned around one last time to see where Billy and the others were. Lonnie and Larry were nowhere in sight. Billy was coming down the hill, his legs trying to keep up with the pedals. I turned and started down the second hill, the thrill of victory already surging through my body.

Before I knew it I was pulling into my driveway. I walked to the garden hose and let the water run over my head, down my neck, and into my boots. I took a long drink and then I sat down underneath the maple tree to wait.

I waited forever. I actually began to wonder if something had happened. Then finally Larry came slowly down the road. He was matted with sweat and he didn't say a word 'til he had gotten a drink and doused himself with water.

"Where's Billy?" I askcd, incredulous. "And where's Lonnie?'

"Lonnie got so tired," began Larry, still breathing hard "...that he told me to go ahead. I think he probably went home. He was really beat."

"What about Billy?" I asked. "I saw him going down the first of those last three hills. Did you pass him?"

"You'll never believe it, Jay," said Larry as he sat down. He paused, shaking his head. "I was coming around the corner before that first big hill at the end. Billy had just started on his way up when he slammed on his brakes and came to a stop. You were so far ahead I couldn't see you. Billy looked around and I guess he didn't see me. He lifted his bike up over his head and slammed into to a fence post. Then he sat down next to it."

My eyes were wide as Larry continued. "When I caught up to Billy and asked him what was wrong, he told me his bike broke down and that he couldn't finish the race. He said he was just about to catch up with you and he pretended to be so mad at his bike."

"You're kidding," I said. Larry was right. It was hard to believe that Billy had smashed his own bike just to have an excuse for not finishing the race. I shook my head.

Larry leaned over and grabbed me by the shoulders. "You did it!" he shook me enthusiastically. "You and *Big Red* beat Billy! I honestly didn't think you would. That bike is sure something."

We gloated for the next few minutes as I explained to Larry how I had watched Billy sweat like a pig while I cruised along behind him waiting to make my move. We laughed.

"I guess *hunt and run* will have to wait 'til next week," I told Larry, "...if Billy can get his bike working by then." We laughed again.

My mom came outside and said Larry's mom had called him home for lunch, so we slapped each other on the back and exchanged our secret handshake. I was ready for lunch too. Then I had another lawn to mow and a few Saturday chores to complete before my papers arrived.

I didn't see Billy for days. The subject of the race never came up and of course I never got Billy's new baseball glove.

Larry

Chapter 15
Larry

The guys had been taking the go-cart out several times a week and every time they went they came to see if I could go with them. Each time I had to say *"no"* it got harder.

It was Saturday morning and Larry rode up to the house as I was pushing the mower back into the garage.

"Hey Jay, we're heading to the school with the go-cart. Can you come? Looks like your mowing is done, and there's still plenty of time before your papers get here."

Just then my dad walked around the corner into the garage.

"Hi Mr. Tims," said Larry. I came by to see if Jay could go with us. We're going over to the school with the go-cart."

My dad liked Larry. Larry was always so polite. Dad smiled as he leaned up against the car and responded to Larry's question. "We're on our way in a few minutes to see Jay's grandma. We don't see much of him these days and his mother made it very clear that he's coming with us on this visit."

"Oh, come on, dad. Can't I go? I haven't been on the go-cart in weeks."

"Sorry son," my dad was apologetic, "but you know that when your mother makes up her mind, there's no other option." He picked up a can of oil and lifted the hood of the car. In a muffled voice he said, "Best get in the house and wash up. It's time we left."

Disappointed, Larry turned around and picked up his bike. He lifted his leg over the bar and as he slipped onto the seat, he put his hands in the center of the handle-bars. He raised his head and said, "I kinda miss having you around, Jay. It's not as much fun, you know. Billy is always pushing us around and Lonnie doesn't say much—but he does have the go-cart so ...you know."

"Yea, I know, Larry," I replied. "I wish I could come but ...well, my grandma is getting pretty old. My mom says I hardly know her." And I gotta get this bike paid for. I signed a contract with Mr. Paterson so I have to stick with it."

Larry reached out for the handlebars of his bike. "Maybe we can get together tonight after you do your papers.... Hey, I know what! I'll come over and help you. That way you can be done early. Sound good?"

"That would be so cool, and I'll let you ride my bike."

Larry frowned. "Yea, right. Like that's going to happen. You won't even let any of us touch it without wiping our fingerprints with that silly red rag of yours." Laughing, he turned his bike around and headed down the driveway. "See you tonight!"

"See you... Really, Larry, I'll let you ride my bike!" I hollered after him.

Larry had always been my best friend. It was good to hear that he missed me because he had no idea how much I had missed him. In the days that followed, I came to realize how much a part of my life our friendship had been and that it was one of those things that could never be replaced.

We arrived home at 4:00 that afternoon. The papers were sitting in the driveway and I had to move them so my dad could drive into the garage. He lifted the garage door and I grabbed the box of rubber bands to get started on the papers. One at a time I rolled and rubber-banded them. After every few papers I looked up hoping to see Larry riding up to help. I could always depend on Larry. When he said he would do something he always followed through. That's one reason I knew he could understand about my commitment to Mr. Paterson.

The papers were almost rolled. *Where is Larry?* I thought to myself as I took another long look down the street. *It's not like him to forget.*

Just then my mom and dad came out of the house. My mom had tears streaming down her face and my dad looked scared. His face was so white that it scared me.

"What's wrong?" I asked. "Is grandma ok?"

Mom came and leaned over, putting one hand on each side of my face. "Something has happened Jay; something very bad. We just got a phone call. There's been an accident and one of your friends was involved."

I didn't need to ask. I knew it was Larry. That's why he hadn't shown up.

"It was Larry wasn't it?" I asked slowly, not knowing how to respond.

"Yes," my mom said, in a barely audible whisper. Then she fell silent.

I knew she wasn't telling me everything, and the sick feeling in my stomach told me why. *Oh no,* I thought. Tears began to cloud my eyes. "He's dead isn't he?" I looked up into my mothers eyes. All she could do was nod her head.

Shock rippled through my body and I started to shake. Mom's hands were shaking too as she sat down on the ground next to me. Dad sat down in front of me with his legs crossed. Leaning toward me, his strong arms reached around and pulled me in close.

"He was in the go-cart—they'd taken it in the street," my dad explained to me.

No one said a word as I let the tears fall. Eventually my body quit shaking and the sobbing gave way to a gentle flow of tears that wouldn't stop.

I don't remember much about the rest of the evening. I think my dad and my sister did my paper route. I cried myself to sleep and I had a dream—so vivid—I can remember it to this day: *I was sitting on the ground doing my papers. I turned and there was Larry next to me handing me the papers. He smiled and said. "Sorry I'm late Jay, but for some reason I can't stay. I just wanted to tell you that it's okay, and that you will always be my best friend."*

Before I could say a word he was gone. I woke up sobbing in my pillow. It was so like Larry to make sure I knew he hadn't forgotten. As I laid there crying, it hit me. I was never going to see my friend again. There would be no more rides down the old dusty railroad trail together. No more frog hunting or baseball games. He would not be there swinging off the big cottonwood tree or sharing the cookies his mom had made when we snuck into the drive in theater. Who would take his streets for *hit and run fun day* to collect pop bottles? Nothing would be the same.

For three days I cried.

I visited Larry's mom and dad when I felt like I could go without crying. Just being in Larry's house was hard. We arrived later in the day as the shadows were creeping across the road. Cars from friends were parked along the front of the house.

Larry's dad was not doing very well. I saw him in the garage as we walked up. He was drinking something from a bottle in a brown paper bag and he was throwing things. My dad sent me into the house with mom and he went into the garage to talk with Larry's dad.

Billy lived across the street from Larry. He was sitting by himself on the curb kicking rocks with one foot and throwing grass into the wind. He looked completely oblivious to all that was going on. I waved as we passed and he waved back. There was a lady at the door with a large dinner dish in her hands. She had a funny-looking hat that reminded me of a dead bird. That would have made Larry laugh. His mom always made fun of people's strange hats. Today I don't think she noticed as she let the lady with the food and the funny hat into the house.

We waited until Larry's mom had finished talking to the lady with dinner. When she left Larry's mom greeted us. She looked down at me and that was all it took. I started to cry. I just couldn't hold back the tears. She was so kind. She reached out and wrapped her arms around me pulling me deep into her apron. I heard her simper as she softly cried with me. She held me for a long time and then we slowly parted. Wiping my eyes with the back of my hand, I tried to say something but nothing came out. She looked down at me and in a soft voice she said, "I know Jay, I know you loved him. I know."

I turned away as a new stream of tears burst from my eyes. I ran out the house and around the corner. The sun was setting as I sat down against the house with my knees pulled up and my forehead pressing against them. I hoped my parents would take their time and give me a chance to recover.

I heard a noise and lifted my head to see who had found me. It was Lonnie. I moved to let him sit down. "Are your parents here too?" he asked.

I nodded, "Yours?" I asked weakly.

"They just went inside," he said with a hoarse voice. I could tell he'd been crying too, so there was no need to hide my face. "They wanted me to go with them but I can't. I can't go in there."

"I know," I said, "just seeing his mom made me cry. I had to leave."

Lonnie was quiet for a minute; then it came gushing out of him. "Billy says it's all my fault!"

"Billy said what?" I asked incredulous. "Billy is mean. Don't listen to him." I tried to comfort Lonnie. "It's not your fault, Lonnie," I told him. "How many times did your dad tell us to stay off the road?"

I had never heard exactly what happened. All I knew was that Larry had been hit by a truck while he was in the go-cart. I knew he was in the road so I knew he wasn't following the rules.

Lonnie was silent for a long time. "What if it *was* my fault?" Lonnie asked quietly as he stared at his feet.

I didn't know what to say. Finally I asked. "What happened?"

Lonnie looked across the road at Billy sitting on the curb. "He really makes me mad, you know! He just thinks he's so tough."

"That's the way he is, Lonnie," I said. "Don't let it get to you."

I knew something was on Lonnie's mind and that it was hard for him to talk. I guessed that if he wanted to get something off his chest he would. We just sat there for the longest time.

"I told him it was all clear," Lonnie finally offered in a voice so faint I could barely hear him.

"What do you mean?" I asked. "Clear for what?"

Lonnie took a deep breath. I could see how painful it was for him. He began. "We wanted to see how fast it would go down a hill. So we took it across the street and up the hill. We'd all done it a couple of times. One of us stood at the bottom to make sure no cars were coming. When the coast was clear, we hollered, 'All clear!' and the one in the cart took off." Lonnie paused and put his face in his hands. "I didn't see the truck. I swear I didn't see it! All of a sudden it was barreling down the road and I yelled to Larry to stop but he was going too fast and he couldn't stop or he didn't' hear me ...I don't' know." Tears were streaming down Lonnie's face, and I felt terrible for him.

"Is it my fault Larry's dead?" he asked. "Is it my fault?"

I was stunned. I had no idea and I didn't know what to tell Lonnie. In a way I thought it *was* his fault and I could see why he felt so awful. But in another way, Larry had chosen to break the rules. It was Larry's decision to ride the cart in the street, and that's what I finally told Lonnie. It seemed to help that I didn't blame him. He took a deep breath and stopped crying.

"It was Billy's idea in the first place," Lonnie added a minute later. "Neither of us wanted to in the beginning. We knew it was against the rules and we told him so but he said we were babies."

That's when I knew exactly what had happened and it made perfect sense to me that Billy was trying to place the blame on Lonnie. It had been Billy's idea in the first place and just like Billy, he had bullied them until they gave in. Billy was the one with the guilty conscience.

I didn't see much of Billy after that. He got into trouble and was sent to live with relatives for the rest of the summer. When he came back it was like we were strangers. Lonnie just kind of faded away. I hardly saw him for the rest of the summer. Things were never the same between us and we never said another word about Larry.

PURCHASE CONTRACT

This contract is _____ ___cle Shop and <u>Mr. Jay Tims</u> for the

sum of $129___ ___ the purchase of a red Schwinn, Mark II

Jaguar ___ ___ #4485492.

Mr. Ti___ ___ <u>$38.75</u> with a balance due of $___.

Pay ___ ___ ___ined by Mr. Tims' weekly earnings until

the bo___ ___

T___ ___ ___ will be owned by Paterson Schwinn Bicycle shop until

such time as the ___ ___ is paid in full.

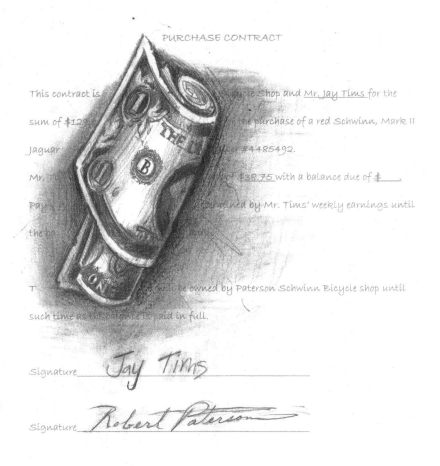

Signature ___ *Jay Tims* _____

Signature ___ *Robert Paterson* _____

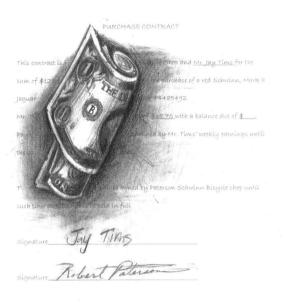

PURCHASE CONTRACT

This contract is _____ Shop and Mr. Jay Tims for the
sum of $12 _____ purchase of a red Schwinn, Mark II
Jaguar _____ #4485492.
Mr. _____ $8.75 with a balance due of $____
Pay _____ by Mr. Tims' weekly earnings until
the _____
T _____ owned by Paterson Schwinn Bicycle shop until
such time _____ paid in full.

Signature _Jay Tims_____

Signature _Robert Paterson_____

Chapter 16
Pay Off

I wanted the world to stop and let me off but I had responsibilities. The sun still came up every morning. The birds still sang and the grass continued to grow—and I had committed to cut it. Life went on as usual. Although I didn't sell spudnuts for a week or shine any shoes, and although Mr. Jepson let me have a week off delivering door hangers, I kept up with my lawn mowing and of course the newspapers had to be delivered every day. The first week was the worst and then things gradually got a little easier. Time has a way of easing pain but sometimes it passes slowly.

I made my weekly trips to see Mr. Paterson. Each week brought me closer to the final pay off. The summer was nearly over when I made my last payment.

I counted out the last of the money I owed Mr. Paterson. I rolled it up and put it in my pocket. Then I opened the garage and brought out the Big Red Bike. It was still my pride and joy, and thanks to Mr. Paterson I knew how to take good care of it. Today, more than any other day, I wanted him to see it all polished and shining when I made my last payment.

I spent more than an hour cleaning it. I buffed the chrome fenders. I polished the paint 'til I was sure I could see the reflection of the cars passing in the road— just like the day I had seen it for the first time. I greased the chain and I even shined the spokes. I was sure it looked dazzling as I rode to the bike shop.

After so many trips to the bike shop, it felt like my second home. When I arrived, Mr. Paterson was sitting on a chair in the back of the shop talking on the phone. He looked up and waved for me to come back. The door slammed as the air from the air conditioner forced it shut. The smell of grease and leather permeated the air. (To this day the smell of a bike shop makes me feel like a kid again.) I noticed that Mr. Paterson had placed the latest new bicycle in the front window. It was nothing like my Big Red Bike.

I walked to the counter with my hand in my pocket holding onto the roll of bills. I thought about all the hard work I had done to get to this place—all the time running from house to house, mowing lawns, selling spudnuts, shining shoes, pulling weeds, and delivering papers. It had been a long summer and yet now that it was over I felt like it had raced past. School would start in a couple of weeks and this summer would be history.

Mr. Paterson finished up on the phone and slid over to the fridge on his rolling chair. He pulled out two bottles of soda. I took one and opened it with a quick snap using the opener on the end of the counter.

"Well, Mr. Paterson, today is the big day," I said. I reached deep into my pocket and pulled out the roll of bills. I laid it on the counter with a smile.

He leaned over and rested his head on his hands, "So this is the big day is it?" Sitting up, he looked down at the roll of cash, picked it up and dropped it in the drawer behind the counter. He didn't bother to count it. He pulled out his accounting book and opened it up to the page with my name on it. He wrote, "PAID IN FULL," then placed the book back in the drawer.

I took a deep breath and let it out all at once. The bike was completely mine. I had done it!

Mr. Paterson laughed when I let out the sigh. "You've accomplished an awesome thing, Jay," he said to me. "And this is just the beginning. Remember there is no dream too big when you work hard and believe."

That was one of the lessons I had learned during the summer. I had discovered for myself that if you really wanted something and were totally committed to it, the way to make it happen would open in front of you.

I spent several hours with Mr. Paterson that afternoon. I'd already mowed my lawns for the day and I wasn't selling spudnuts anymore or shining shoes. I had also quit the not so fun and run job in the early mornings. I helped Mr. Paterson put a couple of bikes together and we talked about a lot of things.

When I got ready to leave he said, "Don't make yourself scarce, Jay. I've really enjoyed our talks and I hope you'll come and visit me whenever you can."

"Oh, I will," I said enthusiastically. "I'll come back every chance I get." I was glad he wanted me to come back. Mr. Paterson had become my friend. That was the other thing I had learned during the summer—the value of a good friend.

In the beginning I visited Mr. Paterson every week or two but the visits got to be fewer and farther between as I grew older. Four years after I bought the Big Red Bike, Mr. Paterson closed

the Schwinn bike shop and moved away. I never
heard from him again.

Epilogue

Twenty years later as an industrial salesman, I was making cold calls in the Salt Lake City area. I walked into a copy machine business to offer my company's services and was invited into the president's office to make my sales pitch.

The office overlooked the city from an expansive picture window. On the far wall was a costly bookshelf with a variety of books and memorabilia. The older man at the desk was obviously a very successful businessman. On the front of his desk was his name:

MR. ROBERT PATERSON
PRESIDENT/CEO

Just the name brought back memories. I interrupted his concentration as he reviewed several files at his desk. "You know," I said, "I once knew a man with the very same name as yours. He was a very good friend."

He looked up over his glasses and reached out as I handed him my business card. Glancing at my name he stood as quickly as a man of his years could get up.

"Do you know who I am?" he asked. With open arms, he hurried around his desk and gave me the biggest hug. Without a word we held each other. "I remember you so well," he said, "and I remember the talks we had every Friday when you came into the shop."

I couldn't believe it was happening—after all these years. So many times I had wanted to tell him how much of a difference he had made in my life. I had wanted him to know what an influence he had been and how grateful I was. I was finally being offered the opportunity to tell him. We sat down and talked and laughed.

"How are your folks, Jay," he asked after a few minutes.

"I lost my dad two years ago—a heart attack," I told him.

He was sad to hear the news but then a small smile crossed his lips and he said, "I have a confession to share with you. I promised your dad way back when you bought that bike that I wouldn't tell you this, but since he's gone and under the circumstances I don't think he would mind anyway."

He swiveled his chair around and reaching down, he opened a small refrigerator behind his desk. He drew out two bottles of orange soda. Then sliding his chair to the side of his desk he popped the tops off using an old fashioned pop bottle opener that was attached underneath his desk.

I laughed out loud. It was just like old times; the memories came flooding back. Not much had changed in the world of Mr. Robert Paterson.

He leaned back in his chair and took a sip of soda. Then he bent forward, put his bottle down and began his confession. "Your dad called me that first night after we made our deal on the bike. Did you know that?"

"No," I said, "I had no idea. He never said a word to me."

Robert smiled and continued, "He was so proud of you for your determination and he could see how hard you were willing to work for the bike. Both of us were pretty impressed. You were only 9 years old. Your dad didn't want to dampen your enthusiasm or spoil the arrangement we had made. But, you know how your father was. He never asked anyone for anything that he couldn't pay for. The following Monday he walked into the shop with your mother. He handed me an envelope from the First National Bank of Layton. Inside was a $100.00 bill. He told me that he wanted to make sure the bike was paid for. Then he asked me to hold onto the payments you made each week and to give them to him at church so he could pay back the loan."

I was speechless. I had no idea. I reflected on how difficult times had been when I was a kid. I remembered how hard my mom and dad had worked to pay off the little house they owned so they could retire without any debt. It was a big deal for my dad to have gotten a loan—even for that small amount. It made me appreciate them even more.

Mr. Paterson continued. "I remember your dad was so surprised when I gave him the first two payments you made. They were sizable payments— much more than either of us had expected and much more than he needed to make the payment at the bank. He was proud. I was proud and you weren't even my son."

Mr. Paterson and I traded a few more memories and I had the chance to tell him how much he had influenced my life—teaching me to pursue my dreams. I was grateful for the opportunity to tell him, and I hoped that in some small way it would repay him for all the things he had taught me.

At the door on my way out I turned around to ask if we could meet for lunch sometime. He had opened his drawer and pulled out a red shop towel. He was wiping the water from his desk where my pop bottle had been sitting. I laughed again—but this time to myself.

When he had finished I asked, "Could I interest you in a lunch date in a couple of weeks?"

He looked up and said, "That would be wonderful, Jay. I'd like that very much. Give me a call when you have the time."

I went out the door not knowing that it would be the last time I would see him. Just a few weeks later I picked up the paper while waiting for a breakfast meeting and saw his name and picture in the obituaries. Just like he had left Layton when I was a boy, he had left this world.

I attended the funeral and had the chance to meet Robert's children afterward. I shared the story of the Big Red Bike. They had never heard it. I discovered that mine was one of many stories his children had heard that day. Evidently Robert Paterson had influenced quite a few people during his life—quietly teaching them to believe in themselves and in their dreams.

I knew it had been no accident that I had had the chance to meet Mr. Paterson again after so many years. There are no accidents. There is no chance or fate. There is only what we create when we decide to pursue our dreams. I was glad I had come to understand that as a 9-year-old boy.